Jeeves in the Springtime

& Other Stories

P. G. WODEHOUSE

The Manor Wodehouse Collection

TARK CLASSIC FICTION
AN IMPRINT OF

MANOR
Rockville, Maryland
2008

ISBN: 978-1-60450-057-8

Published by TARK Classic Fiction
An Imprint of Arc Manor
P. O. Box 10339
Rockville, MD 20849-0339
www.ArcManor.com

Printed in the United States of America/United Kingdom

Contents

Please Visit

www.ManorWodehouse.com

for a complete list of titles available in our
Manor Wodehouse Collection

DEATH AT THE EXCELSIOR

THE room was the typical bedroom of the typical boarding-house, furnished, insofar as it could be said to be furnished at all, with a severe simplicity. It contained two beds, a pine chest of drawers, a strip of faded carpet, and a wash basin. But there was that on the floor which set this room apart from a thousand rooms of the same kind. Flat on his back, with his hands tightly clenched and one leg twisted oddly under him and with his teeth gleaming through his grey beard in a horrible grin, Captain John Gunner stared up at the ceiling with eyes that saw nothing.

Until a moment before, he had had the little room all to himself. But now two people were standing just inside the door, looking down at him. One was a large policeman, who twisted his helmet nervously in his hands. The other was a tall, gaunt old woman in a rusty black dress, who gazed with pale eyes at the dead man. Her face was quite expressionless.

The woman was Mrs. Pickett, owner of the Excelsior Boarding-House. The policeman's name was Grogan. He was a genial giant, a terror to the riotous element of the waterfront, but obviously ill at ease in the presence of death. He drew in his breath, wiped his forehead, and whispered: "Look at his eyes, ma'am!"

Mrs. Pickett had not spoken a word since she had brought the policeman into the room, and she did not do so now. Constable Grogan looked at her quickly. He was afraid of Mother Pickett, as was everybody else along the waterfront. Her silence, her pale eyes, and the quiet decisiveness of her personality cowed even the tough old salts who patronized the Excelsior. She was a formidable influence in that little community of sailormen.

"That's just how I found him," said Mrs. Pickett. She did not speak loudly, but her voice made the policeman start.

He wiped his forehead again. "It might have been apoplexy," he hazarded.

Mrs. Pickett said nothing. There was a sound of footsteps outside, and a young man entered, carrying a black bag.

"Good morning, Mrs. Pickett. I was told that – Good Lord!" The young doctor dropped to his knees beside the body and raised one of the arms. After a moment he lowered it gently to the floor, and shook his head in grim resignation.

"He's been dead for hours," he announced. "When did you find him?"

"Twenty minutes back," replied the old woman. "I guess he died last night. He never would be called in the morning. Said he liked to sleep on. Well, he's got his wish."

"What did he die of, sir?" asked the policeman.

"It's impossible to say without an examination," the doctor answered. "It looks like a stroke, but I'm pretty sure it isn't. It might be a coronary attack, but I happen to know his blood pressure was normal, and his heart sound. He called in to see me only a week ago, and I examined him thoroughly. But sometimes you can be deceived. The inquest will tell us." He eyed the body almost resentfully. "I can't understand it. The man had no right to drop dead like this. He was a tough old sailor who ought to have been good for another twenty years. If you want my honest opinion – though I can't possibly be certain until after the inquest – I should say he had been poisoned."

"How would he be poisoned?" asked Mrs. Pickett quietly.

"That's more than I can tell you. There's no glass about that he could have drunk it from. He might have got it in capsule form. But why should he have done it? He was always a pretty cheerful sort of old man, wasn't he?"

"Yes, sir," said the Constable. "He had the name of being a joker in these parts. Kind of sarcastic, they tell me, though he never tried it on me."

"He must have died quite early last night," said the doctor. He turned to Mrs. Pickett. "What's become of Captain Muller? If he shares this room he ought to be able to tell us something about it."

"Captain Muller spent the night with some friends at Portsmouth," said Mrs. Pickett. "He left right after supper, and hasn't returned."

The doctor stared thoughtfully about the room, frowning.

"I don't like it. I can't understand it. If this had happened in India I should have said the man had died from some form of snakebite. I was out there two years, and I've seen a hundred cases of it. The poor devils all looked just like this. But the thing's ridiculous. How could a man be bitten by a snake in a Southampton waterfront boarding-house? Was the door locked when you found him, Mrs. Pickett?"

Mrs. Pickett nodded. "I opened it with my own key. I had been calling to him and he didn't answer, so I guessed something was wrong."

The Constable spoke: "You ain't touched anything, ma'am? They're always very particular about that. If the doctor's right, and there's been anything up, that's the first thing they'll ask."

"Everything's just as I found it."

"What's that on the floor beside him?" the doctor asked.

"Only his harmonica. He liked to play it of an evening in his room. I've had some complaints about it from some of the gentlemen, but I never saw any harm, so long as he didn't play it too late."

"Seems as if he was playing it when – it happened," Constable Grogan said. "That don't look much like suicide, sir."

"I didn't say it was suicide."

Grogan whistled. "You don't think—"

"I'm not thinking anything – until after the inquest. All I say is that it's queer."

Another aspect of the matter seemed to strike the policeman. "I guess this ain't going to do the Excelsior any good, ma'am," he said sympathetically.

Mrs. Pickett shrugged her shoulders.

"I suppose I had better go and notify the coroner," said the doctor.

He went out, and after a momentary pause the policeman followed him. Constable Grogan was not greatly troubled with nerves, but he felt a decided desire to be somewhere where he could not see the dead man's staring eyes.

Mrs. Pickett remained where she was, looking down at the still form on the floor. Her face was expressionless, but inwardly she was tormented and alarmed. It was the first time such a thing as this had happened at the Excelsior, and, as Constable Grogan had hinted, it was not likely to increase the attractiveness of the house in the eyes of possible boarders. It was not the threatened pecuniary loss which was troubling her. As far as money was concerned, she could have lived comfortably on her savings, for she was richer than most of her friends supposed. It was the blot on the escutcheon of the Excelsior – the stain on its reputation – which was tormenting her.

The Excelsior was her life. Starting many years before, beyond the memory of the oldest boarder, she had built up the model establishment, the fame of which had been carried to every corner of the world. Men spoke of it as a place where you were fed well, cleanly housed, and where petty robbery was unknown.

Such was the chorus of praise that it is not likely that much harm could come to the Excelsior from a single mysterious death but Mother Pickett was not consoling herself with such reflections.

She looked at the dead man with pale, grim eyes. Out in the hallway the doctor's voice further increased her despair. He was talking to the police on the telephone, and she could distinctly hear his every word.

II

The offices of Mr. Paul Snyder's Detective Agency in New Oxford Street had grown in the course of a dozen years from a single room to an impressive suite bright with polished wood, clicking typewriters, and other evidences of success. Where once Mr. Snyder had sat and waited for clients and attended to them himself, he now sat in his private office and directed eight assistants.

He had just accepted a case – a case that might be nothing at all or something exceedingly big. It was on the latter possibility that he had gambled. The fee offered was, judged by his present standards of prosperity, small. But the bizarre facts, coupled with something in the personality of the client, had won him over. He briskly touched the bell and requested that Mr. Oakes should be sent in to him.

Elliot Oakes was a young man who both amused and interested Mr. Snyder, for though he had only recently joined the staff, he made no secret of his intention of revolutionizing the methods of the agency. Mr. Snyder himself, in common with most of his assistants, relied for results on hard work and plenty of common sense. He had never been a detective of the showy type. Results had justified his methods, but he was perfectly aware that young Mr. Oakes looked on him as a dull old man who had been miraculously favored by luck.

Mr. Snyder had selected Oakes for the case in hand principally because it was one where inexperience could do no harm, and where the brilliant guesswork which Oakes preferred to call his inductive reasoning might achieve an unexpected success.

Another motive actuated Mr. Snyder in his choice. He had a strong suspicion that the conduct of this case was going to have the beneficial result of lowering Oakes' self-esteem. If failure achieved this end, Mr. Snyder felt that failure, though it would not help the Agency, would not be an unmixed ill.

The door opened and Oakes entered tensely. He did everything tensely, partly from a natural nervous energy, and partly as a pose. He was a lean young man, with dark eyes and a thin-lipped mouth, and he looked quite as much like a typical detective as Mr. Snyder looked like a comfortable and prosperous stock broker.

"Sit down, Oakes," said Mr. Snyder. "I've got a job for you."

Oakes sank into a chair like a crouching leopard, and placed the tips of his fingers together. He nodded curtly. It was part of his pose to be keen and silent.

"I want you to go to this address" – Mr. Snyder handed him an envelope – "and look around. The address on that envelope is of a sailors' boarding-house down in Southampton. You know the sort of place – retired sea captains and so on live there. All most respectable. In all its history nothing more sensational has ever happened than a case of suspected cheating at halfpenny nap. Well, a man had died there."

"Murdered?" Oakes asked.

"I don't know. That's for you to find out. The coroner left it open. 'Death by Misadventure' was the verdict, and I don't blame him. I don't see how it could have been murder. The door was locked on the inside, so nobody could have got in."

"The window?"

"The window was open, granted. But the room is on the second floor. Anyway, you may dismiss the window. I remember the old lady saying there was a bar across it, and that nobody could have squeezed through."

Oakes' eyes glistened. He was interested. "What was the cause of death?" he asked.

Mr. Snyder coughed. "Snake bite," he said.

Oakes' careful calm deserted him. He uttered a cry of astonishment. "Why, that's incredible!"

"It's the literal truth. The medical examination proved that the fellow had been killed by snake poison – cobra, to be exact, which is found principally in India."

"Cobra!"

"Just so. In a Southampton boarding-house, in a room with a locked door, this man was stung by a cobra. To add a little mystification to the limpid simplicity of the affair, when the door was opened there was no sign of any cobra. It couldn't have got out through the door, because the door was locked. It couldn't have got out of the window, because the window was too high up, and snakes can't jump. And it couldn't have gotten up the chimney, because there was no chimney. So there you have it."

He looked at Oakes with a certain quiet satisfaction. It had come to his ears that Oakes had been heard to complain of the infantile nature and unworthiness of the last two cases to which he had been assigned. He had even said that he hoped some day to be given a problem which should be beyond the reasoning powers of a child of six. It seemed to Mr. Snyder that Oakes was about to get his wish.

"I should like further details," said Oakes, a little breathlessly.

"You had better apply to Mrs. Pickett, who owns the boarding-house," Mr. Snyder said. "It was she who put the case in my hands. She is convinced that it is murder. But, if we exclude ghosts, I don't see how any third party could have taken a hand in the thing at all. However, she wanted a man from this agency, and was prepared to pay for him, so I promised her I would send one. It is not our policy to turn business away."

He smiled wryly. "In pursuance of that policy I want you to go and put up at Mrs. Pickett's boarding house and do your best to enhance the reputation of our agency. I would suggest that you pose as a ship's chandler or something of that sort. You will have to be something maritime or they'll be suspicious of you. And if your visit produces no other results, it will, at least, enable you to make the acquaintance of a very remarkable woman. I commend Mrs. Pickett to your notice. By the way, she says she will help you in your investigations."

Oakes laughed shortly. The idea amused him.

"It's a mistake to scoff at amateur assistance, my boy," said Mr. Snyder in the benevolently paternal manner which had made a score of criminals refuse to believe him a detective until the moment when the handcuffs snapped on their wrists. "Crime investigation isn't an exact science. Success or failure depends in a large measure on applied common sense, and the possession of a great deal of special information. Mrs. Pickett knows certain things which neither you nor I know, and it's just possible that she may have some stray piece of information which will provide the key to the entire mystery."

Oakes laughed again. "It is very kind of Mrs. Pickett," he said, "but I prefer to trust to my own methods." Oakes rose, his face purposeful. "I'd better be starting at once," he said. "I'll send you reports from time to time."

"Good. The more detailed the better," said Mr. Snyder genially. "I hope your visit to the Excelsior will be pleasant. And cultivate Mrs. Pickett. She's worth while."

The door closed, and Mr. Snyder lighted a fresh cigar. "Dashed young fool," he murmured, as he turned his mind to other matters.

III

A day later Mr. Snyder sat in his office reading a typewritten report. It appeared to be of a humorous nature, for, as he read, chuckles escaped him. Finishing the last sheet he threw his head back and laughed heartily. The manuscript had not been intended by its author for a humorous effort. What Mr. Snyder had been reading was the first of Elliott Oakes' reports from the Excelsior. It read as follows:

I am sorry to be unable to report any real progress. I have formed several theories which I will put forward later, but at present I cannot say that I am hopeful.

Directly I arrived here I sought out Mrs. Pickett, explained who I was, and requested her to furnish me with any further information which might be of service to me. She is a strange, silent woman, who impressed me as having very little intelligence. Your suggestion that I should avail myself of her assistance seems more curious than ever, now that I have seen her.

The whole affair seems to me at the moment of writing quite inexplicable. Assuming that this Captain Gunner was murdered, there appears to have been no motive for the crime whatsoever. I have made careful inquiries about him, and find that he was a man of fifty-five; had spent nearly forty years of his life at sea, the last dozen in command of his own ship; was of a somewhat overbearing disposition, though with a fund of rough humour; had travelled all over the world, and had been an inmate of the Excelsior for about ten months. He had a small annuity, and no other money at all, which disposes of money as the motive for the crime.

In my character of James Burton, a retired ship's chandler, I have mixed with the other boarders, and have heard all they have to say about the affair. I gather that the deceased was by no means popular. He appears to have had a bitter tongue, and I have not met one man who seems to regret his death. On the other hand, I have heard nothing which would suggest that he had any active and violent enemies. He was simply the unpopular boarder – there is always one in every boarding-house – but nothing more.

I have seen a good deal of the man who shared his room – another sea captain, named Muller. He is a big, silent person, and it is not easy to get him to talk. As regards the death of Captain Gunner he can tell me nothing. It seems that on the night of the tragedy he was away at Portsmouth with some friends. All I have got from him is some information as to Captain Gunner's habits, which leads nowhere. The dead man seldom drank, except at night when he would take some whisky. His head was not strong, and a little of the spirit was enough to make him semi-intoxicated, when he would be hilarious and often insulting. I gather that Muller found him a difficult roommate, but he is one of those placid persons who can put up with anything. He and Gunner were in the habit of playing draughts together every night in their room, and Gunner had a harmonica which he played frequently. Apparently, he was playing it very soon before he died, which is significant, as seeming to dispose of the idea of suicide.

As I say, I have one or two theories, but they are in a very nebulous state. The most plausible is that on one of his visits to India – I have ascertained that he made several voyages there – Captain Gunner may in some way have fallen foul of the natives. The fact that he certainly died of the poison of an Indian snake supports this theory. I am making inquiries as to the movements of several Indian sailors who were here in their ships at the time of the tragedy.

I have another theory. Does Mrs. Pickett know more about this affair than she appears to? I may be wrong in my estimate of her mental qualities. Her apparent stupidity may be cunning. But here again, the absence of motive brings me up against a dead wall. I must confess that at present I do not see my way clearly. However, I will write again shortly.

Mr. Snyder derived the utmost enjoyment from the report. He liked the substance of it, and above all, he was tickled by the bitter tone of frustration which characterized it. Oakes was baffled, and his knowledge of Oakes told him that the sensation of being baffled was gall and wormwood to that high-spirited young man. Whatever might be the result of this investigation, it would teach him the virtue of patience.

He wrote his assistant a short note:

Dear Oakes,

Your report received. You certainly seem to have got the hard case which, I hear, you were pining for. Don't build too much on plausible motives in a case of this sort. Fauntleroy, the London murderer, killed a woman for no other reason than that she had thick ankles. Many years ago, I myself was on a case where a man murdered an intimate friend because of a dispute about a bet. My experience is that five murderers out of ten act on the whim of the moment, without anything which, properly speaking, you could call a motive at all.

Yours very cordially,

Paul Snyder

P. S. I don't think much of your Pickett theory. However, you're in charge. I wish you luck.

IV

Young Mr. Oakes was not enjoying himself. For the first time in his life, the self-confidence which characterized all his actions seemed to be failing him. The change had taken place almost over-night. The fact that the case had the appearance of presenting the unusual had merely stimulated him at first. But then doubts had crept in and the problem had begun to appear insoluble.

True, he had only just taken it up, but something told him that, for all the progress he was likely to make, he might just as well have been working on it steadily for a month. He was completely baffled. And every moment which he spent in the Excelsior Boarding-House made it clearer to him that that infernal old woman with the pale eyes thought him an incompetent fool. It was that, more than any-thing, which made him acutely conscious of his lack of success. His nerves were being sorely troubled by the quiet scorn of Mrs. Pick-ett's gaze. He began to think that perhaps he had been a shade too self-confident and abrupt in the short interview which he had had with her on his arrival.

As might have been expected, his first act, after his brief inter-view with Mrs. Pickett, was to examine the room where the tragedy had taken place. The body was gone, but otherwise nothing had been moved.

Oakes belonged to the magnifying-glass school of detection. The first thing he did on entering the room was to make a careful ex-amination of the floor, the walls, the furniture, and the windowsill. He would have hotly denied the assertion that he did this because it looked well, but he would have been hard put to it to advance any other reason.

If he discovered anything, his discoveries were entirely negative, and served only to deepen the mystery of the case. As Mr. Snyder had said, there was no chimney, and nobody could have entered through the locked door.

There remained the window. It was small, and apprehensiveness, perhaps, of the possibility of burglars, had caused the proprietress to make it doubly secure with an iron bar. No human being could have squeezed his way through it.

It was late that night that he wrote and dispatched to headquar-ters the report which had amused Mr. Snyder.

V

Two days later Mr. Snyder sat at his desk, staring with wide, unbelieving eyes at a telegram he had just received. It read as follows:

Have Solved Gunner Mystery. Returning.... Oakes.

Mr. Snyder narrowed his eyes and rang the bell. "Send Mr. Oakes to me directly he arrives," he said.

He was pained to find that his chief emotion was one of bitter annoyance. The swift solution of such an apparently insoluble problem would reflect the highest credit on the Agency, and there were picturesque circumstances connected with the case which would make it popular with the newspapers and lead to its being given a great deal of publicity.

Yet, in spite of all this, Mr. Snyder was annoyed. He realized now how large a part the desire to reduce Oakes' self-esteem had played with him. He further realized, looking at the thing honestly, that he had been firmly convinced that the young man would not come within a mile of a reasonable solution of the mystery. He had desired only that his failure would prove a valuable educational experience for him. For he believed that failure at this particular point in his career would make Oakes a more valuable asset to the Agency. But now here Oakes was, within a ridiculously short space of time, returning to the fold, not humble and defeated, but triumphant. Mr. Snyder looked forward with apprehension to the young man's probable demeanor under the intoxicating influence of victory.

His apprehensions were well grounded. He had barely finished the third of the series of cigars, which, like milestones, marked the progress of his afternoon, when the door opened and young Oakes entered. Mr. Snyder could not repress a faint moan at the sight of him. One glance was enough to tell him that his worst fears were realised.

"I got your telegram," said Mr. Snyder.

Oakes nodded. "It surprised you, eh?" he asked.

Mr. Snyder resented the patronizing tone of the question, but he had resigned himself to be patronized, and keep his anger in check.

"Yes," he replied, "I must say it did surprise me. I didn't gather from your report that you had even found a clue. Was it the Indian theory that turned the trick?"

Oakes laughed tolerantly. "Oh, I never really believed that preposterous theory for one moment. I just put it in to round out my report. I hadn't begun to think about the case then – not really think."

Mr. Snyder, nearly exploding with wrath, extended his cigar-case. "Light up, and tell me all about it," he said, controlling his anger.

"Well, I won't say I haven't earned this," said Oakes, puffing away. He let the ash of his cigar fall delicately to the floor – another action which seemed significant to his employer. As a rule, his assistants, unless particularly pleased with themselves, used the ashtray.

"My first act on arriving," Oakes said, "was to have a talk with Mrs. Pickett. A very dull old woman."

"Curious. She struck me as rather intelligent."

"Not on your life. She gave me no assistance whatever. I then examined the room where the death had taken place. It was exactly as you described it. There was no chimney, the door had been locked on the inside, and the one window was very high up. At first sight, it looked extremely unpromising. Then I had a chat with some of the other boarders. They had nothing of any importance to contribute. Most of them simply gibbered. I then gave up trying to get help from the outside, and resolved to rely on my own intelligence."

He smiled triumphantly. "It is a theory of mine, Mr. Snyder, which I have found valuable that, in nine cases out of ten, remarkable things don't happen."

"I don't quite follow you there," Mr. Snyder interrupted.

"I will put it another way, if you like. What I mean is that the simplest explanation is nearly always the right one. Consider this case. It seemed impossible that there should have been any reasonable explanation of the man's death. Most men would have worn themselves out guessing at wild theories. If I had started to do that, I should have been guessing now. As it is – here I am. I trusted to my belief that nothing remarkable ever happens, and I won out."

Mr. Snyder sighed softly. Oakes was entitled to a certain amount of gloating, but there could be no doubt that his way of telling a story was downright infuriating.

"I believe in the logical sequence of events. I refuse to accept effects unless they are preceded by causes. In other words, with all due respect to your possibly contrary opinions, Mr. Snyder, I simply decline to believe in a murder unless there was a motive for it. The first thing I set myself to ascertain was – what was the motive for the murder of Captain Gunner? And, after thinking it over and making every possible inquiry, I decided that there was no motive. Therefore, there was no murder."

Mr. Snyder's mouth opened, and he obviously was about to protest. But he appeared to think better of it and Oakes proceeded: "I then tested the suicide theory. What motive was there for suicide? There was no motive. Therefore, there was no suicide."

This time Mr. Snyder spoke. "You haven't been spending the last few days in the wrong house by any chance, have you? You will be telling me next that there wasn't any dead man."

Oakes smiled. "Not at all. Captain John Gunner was dead, all right. As the medical evidence proved, he died of the bite of a cobra. It was a small cobra which came from Java."

Mr. Snyder stared at him. "How do you know?"

"I do know, beyond any possibility of doubt."

"Did you see the snake?"

Oakes shook his head.

"Then, how in heaven's name—"

"I have enough evidence to make a jury convict Mr. Snake without leaving the box."

"Then suppose you tell me this. How did your cobra from Java get out of the room?"

"By the window," replied Oakes, impassively.

"How can you possibly explain that? You say yourself that the window was high up."

"Nevertheless, it got out by the window. The logical sequence of events is proof enough that it was in the room. It killed Captain Gunner there, and left traces of its presence outside. Therefore, as the window was the only exit, it must have escaped by that route. It may have climbed or it may have jumped, but somehow it got out of that window."

"What do you mean – it left traces of its presence outside?"

"It killed a dog in the backyard behind the house," Oakes said. "The window of Captain Gunner's room projects out over it. It is full of boxes and litter and there are a few stunted shrubs scattered about. In fact, there is enough cover to hide any small object like the body of a dog. That's why it was not discovered at first. The maid at the Excelsior came on it the morning after I sent you my report while she was emptying a box of ashes in the yard. It was just an ordinary stray dog without collar or license. The analyst examined the body, and found that the dog had died of the bite of a cobra."

"But you didn't find the snake?"

"No. We cleaned out that yard till you could have eaten your breakfast there, but the snake had gone. It must have escaped through the door of the yard, which was standing ajar. That was a couple of days ago, and there has been no further tragedy. In all likelihood it is dead. The nights are pretty cold now, and it would probably have died of exposure."

"But, I just don't understand how a cobra got to Southampton," said the amazed Mr. Snyder.

"Can't you guess it? I told you it came from Java."

"How did you know it did?"

"Captain Muller told me. Not directly, but I pieced it together from what he said. It seems that an old shipmate of Captain Gunner's was living in Java. They corresponded, and occasionally this man would send the captain a present as a mark of his esteem. The last present he sent was a crate of bananas. Unfortunately, the snake must have got in unnoticed. That's why I told you the cobra was a small one. Well, that's my case against Mr. Snake, and short of catching him with the goods, I don't see how I could have made out a stronger one. Don't you agree?"

It went against the grain for Mr. Snyder to acknowledge defeat, but he was a fair-minded man, and he was forced to admit that Oakes did certainly seem to have solved the impossible.

"I congratulate you, my boy," he said as heartily as he could. "To be completely frank, when you started out, I didn't think you could do it. By the way, I suppose Mrs. Pickett was pleased?"

"If she was, she didn't show it. I'm pretty well convinced she hasn't enough sense to be pleased at anything. However, she has invited me to dinner with her tonight. I imagine she'll be as boring as usual, but she made such a point of it, I had to accept."

VI

For some time after Oakes had gone, Mr. Snyder sat smoking and thinking, in embittered meditation. Suddenly there was brought the card of Mrs. Pickett, who would be grateful if he could spare her a few moments. Mr. Snyder was glad to see Mrs. Pickett. He was a student of character, and she had interested him at their first meeting. There was something about her which had seemed to him unique, and he welcomed this second chance of studying her at close range.

She came in and sat down stiffly, balancing herself on the extreme edge of the chair in which a short while before young Oakes had lounged so luxuriously.

"How are you, Mrs. Pickett?" said Mr. Snyder genially. "I'm very glad that you could find time to pay me a visit. Well, so it wasn't murder after all."

"Sir?"

"I've just been talking to Mr. Oakes, whom you met as James Burton," said the detective. "He has told me all about it."

"He told *me* all about it," said Mrs. Pickett dryly.

Mr. Snyder looked at her inquiringly. Her manner seemed more suggestive than her words.

"A conceited, headstrong young fool," said Mrs. Pickett.

It was no new picture of his assistant that she had drawn. Mr. Snyder had often drawn it himself, but at the present juncture it surprised him. Oakes, in his hour of triumph, surely did not deserve this sweeping condemnation.

"Did not Mr. Oakes' solution of the mystery satisfy you, Mrs. Pickett?"

"No!"

"It struck me as logical and convincing," Mr. Snyder said.

"You may call it all the fancy names you please, Mr. Snyder. But Mr. Oakes' solution was not the right one."

"Have you an alternative to offer?"

Mrs. Pickett tightened her lips.

"If you have, I should like to hear it."

"You will – at the proper time."

"What makes you so certain that Mr. Oakes is wrong?"

"He starts out with an impossible explanation, and rests his whole case on it. There couldn't have been a snake in that room because it couldn't have gotten out. The window was too high."

"But surely the evidence of the dead dog?"

Mrs. Pickett looked at him as if he had disappointed her. "I had always heard *you* spoken of as a man with common sense, Mr. Snyder."

"I have always tried to use common sense."

"Then why are you trying now to make yourself believe that something happened which could not possibly have happened just because it fits in with something which isn't easy to explain?"

"You mean that there is another explanation of the dead dog?" Mr. Snyder asked.

"Not *another*. What Mr. Oakes takes for granted is not an explanation. But there is a common sense explanation, and if he had not been so headstrong and conceited he might have found it."

"You speak as if you had found it," chided Mr. Snyder.

"I have." Mrs. Pickett leaned forward as she spoke, and stared at him defiantly.

Mr. Snyder started. "*You* have?"

"Yes."

"What is it?"

"You will know before tomorrow. In the meantime try and think it out for yourself. A successful and prosperous detective agency like yours, Mr. Snyder, ought to do something in return for a fee."

There was something in her manner so reminiscent of the school teacher reprimanding a recalcitrant pupil that Mr. Snyder's sense of humor came to his rescue. "We do our best, Mrs. Pickett," he said. "But you mustn't forget that we are only human and cannot guarantee results."

Mrs. Pickett did not pursue the subject. Instead, she proceeded to astonish Mr. Snyder by asking him to swear out a warrant for the arrest of a man known to them both on a charge of murder.

Mr. Snyder's breath was not often taken away in his own office. As a rule, he received his clients' communications calmly, strange as they often were. But at her words he gasped. The thought crossed his mind that Mrs. Pickett might well be mentally unbalanced. The details of the case were fresh in his memory, and he distinctly recollected that the person she mentioned had been away from the boarding house on the night of Captain Gunner's death, and could, he imagined, produce witnesses to prove it.

Mrs. Pickett was regarding him with an unfaltering stare. To all outward appearances, she was the opposite of unbalanced.

"But you can't swear out a warrant without evidence," he told her.

"I have evidence," she replied firmly.

"Precisely what kind of evidence?" he demanded.

"If I told you now you would think that I was out of my mind."

"But, Mrs. Pickett, do you realize what you are asking me to do? I cannot make this agency responsible for the arbitrary arrest of a man on the strength of a single individual's suspicions. It might ruin me. At the least it would make me a laughing stock."

"Mr. Snyder, you may use your own judgment whether or not to make the arrest on that warrant. You will listen to what I have to say, and you will see for yourself how the crime was committed. If after that you feel that you cannot make the arrest I will accept your decision. I know who killed Captain Gunner," she said. "I knew it from the beginning. It was like a vision. But I had no proof. Now things have come to light and everything is clear."

Against his judgment, Mr. Snyder was impressed. This woman had the magnetism which makes for persuasiveness.

"It – it sounds incredible." Even as he spoke, he remembered that it had long been a professional maxim of his that nothing was incredible, and he weakened still further.

"Mr. Snyder, I ask you to swear out that warrant."

The detective gave in. "Very well," he said.

Mrs. Pickett rose. "If you will come and dine at my house to-night I think I can prove to you that it will be needed. Will you come?"

"I'll come," promised Mr. Snyder.

VII

When Mr. Snyder arrived at the Excelsior and shortly after he was shown into the little private sitting room where he found Oakes, the third guest of the evening unexpectedly arrived.

Mr. Snyder looked curiously at the newcomer. Captain Muller had a peculiar fascination for him. It was not Mr. Snyder's habit to trust overmuch to appearances. But he could not help admitting that there was something about this man's aspect which brought Mrs. Pickett's charges out of the realm of the fantastic into that of the possible. There was something odd – an unnatural aspect of gloom – about the man. He bore himself like one carrying a heavy burden. His eyes were dull, his face haggard. The next moment the detective was reproaching himself with allowing his imagination to run away with his calmer judgment.

The door opened, and Mrs. Pickett came in. She made no apology for her lateness.

To Mr. Snyder one of the most remarkable points about the dinner was the peculiar metamorphosis of Mrs. Pickett from the brooding silent woman he had known to the gracious and considerate hostess.

Oakes appeared also to be overcome with surprise, so much so that he was unable to keep his astonishment to himself. He had come prepared to endure a dull evening absorbed in grim silence, and he found himself instead opposite a bottle of champagne of a brand and year which commanded his utmost respect. What was even more incredible, his hostess had transformed herself into a pleasant old lady whose only aim seemed to be to make him feel at home.

Beside each of the guests' plates was a neat paper parcel. Oakes picked his up, and stared at it in wonderment. "Why, this is more than a party souvenir, Mrs. Pickett," he said. "It's the kind of mechanical marvel I've always wanted to have on my desk."

"I'm glad you like it, Mr. Oakes," Mrs. Pickett said, smiling. "You must not think of me simply as a tired old woman whom age has completely defeated. I am an ambitious hostess. When I give these little parties, I like to make them a success. I want each of you to remember this dinner."

"I'm sure I will."

Mrs. Pickett smiled again. "I think you all will. You, Mr. Snyder." She paused. "And you, Captain Muller."

To Mr. Snyder there was so much meaning in her voice as she said this that he was amazed that it conveyed no warning to Muller. Captain Muller, however, was already drinking heavily. He looked up when addressed and uttered a sound which might have been taken for an expression of polite acquiescence. Then he filled his glass again.

Mr. Snyder's parcel revealed a watch-charm fashioned in the shape of a tiny, candid-eye camera. "That," said Mrs. Pickett, "is a compliment to your profession." She leaned toward the captain. "Mr. Snyder is a detective, Captain Muller."

He looked up. It seemed to Mr. Snyder that a look of fear lit up his heavy eyes for an instant. It came and went, if indeed it came at all, so swiftly that he could not be certain.

"So?" said Captain Muller. He spoke quite evenly, with just the amount of interest which such an announcement would naturally produce.

"Now for yours, Captain," said Oakes. "I guess it's something special. It's twice the size of mine, anyway."

It may have been something in the old woman's expression as she watched Captain Muller slowly tearing the paper that sent a thrill of excitement through Mr. Snyder. Something seemed to warn him of the approach of a psychological moment. He bent forward eagerly.

There was a strangled gasp, a thump, and onto the table from the captain's hands there fell a little harmonica. There was no mistaking the look on Muller's face now. His cheeks were like wax, and his eyes, so dull till then, blazed with a panic and horror which he could not repress. The glasses on the table rocked as he clutched at the cloth.

Mrs. Pickett spoke. "Why, Captain Muller, has it upset you? I thought that, as his best friend, the man who shared his room, you would value a memento of Captain Gunner. How fond you must have been of him for the sight of his harmonica to be such a shock."

The captain did not speak. He was staring fascinated at the thing on the table. Mrs. Pickett turned to Mr. Snyder. Her eyes, as they met his, held him entranced.

"Mr. Snyder, as a detective, you will be interested in a curious and very tragic affair which happened in this house a few days ago. One of my boarders, Captain Gunner, was found dead in his room. It was the room which he shared with Captain Muller. I am very proud of the reputation of my house, Mr. Snyder, and it was a blow to me that this should have happened. I applied to an agency for a detective, and they sent me a stupid boy, with nothing to recommend him except his belief in himself. He said that Captain Gunner had died by accident, killed by a snake which had come out of a crate of bananas. I knew better. I knew that Captain Gunner had been murdered. Are you listening, Captain Muller? This will interest you, as you were such a friend of his."

The captain did not answer. He was staring straight before him, as if he saw something invisible in eyes forever closed in death.

"Yesterday we found the body of a dog. It had been killed, as Captain Gunner had been, by the poison of a snake. The boy from the agency said that this was conclusive. He said that the snake had escaped from the room after killing Captain Gunner and had in turn killed the dog. I knew that to be impossible, for, if there had been a snake in that room it could not have made its escape."

Her eyes flashed, and became remorselessly accusing. "It was not a snake that killed Captain Gunner. It was a cat. Captain Gunner had a friend who hated him. One day, in opening a crate of bananas, this friend found a snake. He killed it, and extracted the poison. He knew Captain Gunner's habits. He knew that he played a harmonica. This man also had a cat. He knew that cats hated the sound of a harmonica. He had often seen this particular cat fly at Captain Gunner and scratch him when he played. He took the cat and covered its claws with the poison. And then he left it in the room with Captain Gunner. He knew what would happen."

Oakes and Mr. Snyder were on their feet. Captain Muller had not moved. He sat there, his fingers gripping the cloth. Mrs. Pickett rose and went to a closet. She unlocked the door. "Kitty!" she called. "Kitty! Kitty!"

A black cat ran swiftly out into the room. With a clatter and a crash of crockery and a ringing of glass the table heaved, rocked and overturned as Muller staggered to his feet. He threw up his hands as if to ward something off. A choking cry came from his lips. "Gott! Gott!"

Mrs. Pickett's voice rang through the room, cold and biting: "Captain Muller, you murdered Captain Gunner!"

The captain shuddered. Then mechanically he replied: "Gott! Yes, I killed him."

"You heard, Mr. Snyder," said Mrs. Pickett. "He has confessed before witnesses. Take him away."

Muller allowed himself to be moved toward the door. His arm in Mr. Snyder's grip felt limp. Mrs. Pickett stopped and took something from the debris on the floor. She rose, holding the harmonica.

"You are forgetting your souvenir, Captain Muller," she said.

MISUNDERSTOOD

THE profession of Mr. James ("Spider") Buffin was pocket-picking. His hobby was revenge. James had no objection to letting the sun go down on his wrath. Indeed, it was after dark that he corrected his numerous enemies most satisfactorily. It was on a dark night, while he was settling a small score against one Kelly, a mere acquaintance, that he first fell foul of Constable Keating, whose beat took him through the regions which James most frequented.

James, having "laid for" Mr. Kelly, met him in a murky side-street down Clerkenwell way, and attended to his needs with a sandbag.

It was here that Constable Keating first came prominently into his life. Just as James, with the satisfying feeling that his duty had been done, was preparing to depart, Officer Keating, who had been a distant spectator of the affair, charged up and seized him.

It was intolerable that he should interfere in a purely private falling-out between one gentleman and another, but there was nothing to be done. The policeman weighed close upon fourteen stone, and could have eaten Mr. Buffin. The latter, inwardly seething, went quietly, and in due season was stowed away at the Government's expense for the space of sixty days.

Physically, there is no doubt that his detention did him good. The regular hours and the substitution of bread and water for his wonted diet improved his health thirty per cent. It was mentally that he suffered. His was one of those just-as-good cheap-substitute minds, incapable of harbouring more than one idea at a time, and during those sixty days of quiet seclusion it was filled with an ever-growing resentment against Officer Keating. Every day, as he moved about his appointed tasks, he brooded on his wrongs. Every night was to him but the end of another day that kept him from settling down to the serious business of Revenge. To be haled to prison for correcting a private enemy with a sand-bag – that was what stung. In the privacy of his cell he dwelt unceasingly on the necessity for revenge. The thing began to take on to him the aspect almost of a Holy Mission, a sort of Crusade.

The days slipped by, bringing winter to Clerkenwell, and with it Mr. Buffin. He returned to his old haunts one Friday night, thin but in excellent condition. One of the first acquaintances he met was Officer Keating. The policeman, who had a good memory for faces, recognised him, and stopped.

"So you're out, young feller?" he said genially. When not in the active discharge of his professional duties the policeman was a kindly man. He bore Mr. Buffin no grudge.

"Um," said Mr. Buffin.

"Feeling fine, eh?"

"Um."

"Goin' round to see some of the chaps and pass them the time of day, I shouldn't wonder?"

"Um."

"Well, you keep clear of that lot down in Frith Street, young feller. They're no good. And if you get mixed up with them, first thing you know, you'll be in trouble again. And you want to keep out of that now."

"Um."

"If you never get into trouble," said the policeman sententiously, "you'll never have to get out of it."

"Um," said Mr. Buffin. If he had a fault as a conversationalist, it was a certain tendency to monotony, a certain lack of sparkle and variety in his small-talk.

Constable Keating, with a dignified but friendly wave of the hand, as one should say, "You have our leave to depart," went on his way; while Mr. Buffin, raging, shuffled off in the opposite direction, thinking as hard as his limited mental equipment would allow him.

His thoughts, which were many and confused, finally composed themselves into some order. He arrived at a definite conclusion, which was that if the great settlement was to be carried through successfully it must be done when the policeman was off duty. Till then he had pictured himself catching Officer Keating in an unguarded moment on his beat. This, he now saw, was out of the question. On his beat the policeman had no unguarded moments. There was a quiet alertness in his poise, a danger-signal in itself.

There was only one thing for Mr. Buffin to do. Greatly as it would go against the grain, he must foregather with the man, win his confidence, put himself in a position where he would be able to find out what he did with himself when off duty.

The policeman offered no obstacle to the move. A supreme self-confidence was his leading characteristic. Few London policemen are diffident, and Mr. Keating was no exception. It never occurred to him that there could be an ulterior motive behind Mr. Buffin's advances. He regarded Mr. Buffin much as one regards a dog which one has had to chastise. One does not expect the dog to lie in wait and bite. Officer Keating did not expect Mr. Buffin to lie in wait and bite.

So every day, as he strolled on his beat, there sidled up to him the meagre form of Spider Buffin. Every day there greeted him the Spider's "Good-morning, Mr. Keating," till the sight of Officer Keating walking solidly along the pavement with Spider Buffin shuffling along at his side, listening with rapt interest to his views on Life and his hints on Deportment, became a familiar spectacle in Clerkenwell.

Mr. Buffin played his part well. In fact, too well. It was on the seventh day that, sidling along in the direction of his favourite place of refreshment, he found himself tapped on the shoulder. At the same moment an arm, linking itself in his, brought him gently to a halt. Beside him were standing two of the most eminent of the great Frith Street Gang, Otto the Sausage and Rabbit Butler. It was the finger of the Rabbit that had tapped his shoulder. The arm tucked in his was the arm of Otto the Sausage.

"Hi, Spider," said Mr. Butler, "Sid wants to see you a minute."

The Spider's legs felt boneless. There was nothing in the words to alarm a man, but his practised ear had seemed to detect a certain unpleasant dryness in the speaker's tone. Sid Marks, the all-powerful leader of the Frith Street Gang, was a youth whose company the Spider had always avoided with some care.

The great Sid, seated in state at a neighbouring hostelry, fixed his visitor with a cold and questioning eye. Mr. Buffin looked nervous and interrogative. Mr. Marks spoke.

"Your pal Keating pinched Porky Binns this mornin'," said Sid.

The Spider's heart turned to water.

"You and that slop," observed Sid dreamily, "have been bloomin' thick these days."

Mr. Buffin did not affect to misunderstand. Sid Marks was looking at him in that nasty way. Otto the Sausage was looking at him in that nasty way. Rabbit Butler was looking at him in that nasty way. This was an occasion where manly frankness was the quality most to be aimed at. To be misunderstood in the circles in which Mr. Buffin moved meant something more than the mere risk of being treated with cold displeasure.

He began to explain with feverish eagerness.

"Strike me, Sid," he stammered, "it ain't like that. It's all right. Blimey, you don't fink I'm a nark?"

Mr. Marks chewed a straw in silence.

"I'm layin' for him, Sid," babbled Mr. Buffin. "That's true. Strike me if it ain't. I'm just tryin' to find out where he goes when he's off duty. He pinched me, so I'm layin' for him."

Mr. Marks perpended. Rabbit Butler respectfully gave it as his opinion that it would be well to put Mr. Buffin through it. There was nothing like being on the safe side. By putting Mr. Buffin through it, argued Rabbit Butler, they would stand to win either way. If he *had* "smitched" to Officer Keating about Porky Binns he would deserve it. If he had not – well, it would prevent him doing so on some future occasion. Play for safety, was Mr. Butler's advice, seconded by Otto the Sausage. Mr. Buffin, pale to the lips, thought he had never met two more unpleasant persons.

The Great Sid, having chewed his straw for a while in silence, delivered judgment. The prisoner should have the benefit of the doubt this time. His story, however unplausible, might possibly be true. Officer Keating undoubtedly had pinched him. That was in his favour.

"You can hop it this time," he said, "but if you ever do start smitchin', Spider, yer knows what'll happen."

Mr. Buffin withdrew, quaking.

Matters had now come to a head. Unless he very speedily gave proof of his pure and noble intentions, life would become extremely unsafe for him. He must act at once. The thought of what would happen should another of the Frith Streeters be pinched before he, Mr. Buffin, could prove himself innocent of the crime of friendliness with Officer Keating, turned him cold.

Fate played into his hands. On the very next morning Mr. Keating, all unsuspecting, asked him to go to his home with a message for his wife.

"Tell her," said Mr. Keating, "a newspaper gent has given me seats for the play to-night, and I'll be home at a quarter to seven."

Mr. Buffin felt as Cromwell must have felt at Dunbar when the Scots left their stronghold on the hills and came down to the open plain.

The winter had set in with some severity that year, and Mr. Buffin's toes, as he stood in the shadows close to the entrance of the villa where Officer Keating lived when off duty, were soon thoroughly frozen. He did not dare to stamp his feet, for at any moment now the victim might arrive. And when the victim weighs fourteen stone, against the high priest's eight and a half, it behooves the latter to be circumspect, if the sacrifice is to be anything like a success. So Mr. Buffin waited and froze in silence. It was a painful process, and he added it to the black score which already stood against Officer Keating. Never had his thirst for revenge been more tormenting. It is doubtful if a strictly logical and impartial judge would have held Mr. Keating to blame for the fact that Sid Marks' suspicions (and all that those suspicions entailed) had fallen upon Mr. Buffin; but the Spider did so. He felt fiercely resentful against the policeman for placing him in such an unpleasant and dangerous position. As his thoughts ran on the matter, he twisted his fingers tighter round his stick.

As he did so there came from down the road the brisk tramp of feet and a cheerful whistling of "The Wearing of the Green." It is a lugubrious song as a rule, but, as rendered by Officer Keating returning home with theatre tickets, it had all the joyousness of a march-tune.

Every muscle in Mr. Buffin's body stiffened. He gripped his stick and waited. The road was deserted. In another moment....

And then, from nowhere, dark indistinct forms darted out like rats. The whistling stopped in the middle of a bar. A deep-chested oath rang out, and then a confused medley of sound, the rasping of feet, a growling almost canine, a sharp yelp, gasps, and over all the vast voice of Officer Keating threatening slaughter.

For a moment Mr. Buffin stood incapable of motion. The thing had been so sudden, so unexpected. And then, as he realised what was happening, there swept over him in a wave a sense of intolerable injustice. It is not easy to describe his emotions, but they resembled most nearly those of an inventor whose patent has been infringed, or an author whose idea has been stolen. For weeks – and weeks that had seemed like years – he had marked down Officer Keating for his prey. For weeks he had tortured a mind all unused to thinking into providing him with schemes for accomplishing his end. He had outraged his nature by being civil to a policeman. He had risked his life by incurring the suspicions of Sid Marks. He had bought a stick. And he had waited in the cold till his face was blue and his feet blocks of ice. And now ... *now* ... after all this ... a crowd of irresponsible strangers, with no rights in the man whatsoever probably, if the truth were known, filled with mere ignoble desire for his small change, had dared to rush in and jump his claim before his very eyes.

With one passionate cry, Mr. Buffin, forgetting his frozen feet, lifted his stick, and galloped down the road to protect his property....

"That's the stuff," said a voice. "Pour some more into him, Jerry."

Mr. Buffin opened his eyes. A familiar taste was in his mouth. Somebody of liberal ideas seemed to be pouring whisky down his throat. Could this be Heaven? He raised his head, and a sharp pain shot through it. And with the pain came recollection. He remembered now, dimly, as if it had all happened in another life, the mad rush down the road, the momentary pause in the conflict, and then its noisy renewal on a more impressive scale. He remembered striking out left and right with his stick. He remembered the cries of the wounded, the pain of his frozen feet, and finally the crash of something hard and heavy on his head.

He sat up, and found himself the centre of a little crowd. There was Officer Keating, dishevelled but intact; three other policemen, one of whom was kneeling by his side with a small bottle in his hand; and, in the grip of the two were standing two youths.

One was Otto the Sausage; the other was Rabbit Butler.

The kneeling policeman was proffering the bottle once more. Mr. Buffin snatched at it. He felt that it was just what at that moment he needed most.

❦

He did what he could. The magistrate asked for his evidence. He said he had none. He said he thought there must be some mistake. With a twisted smile in the direction of the prisoners, he said that he did not remember having seen either of them at the combat. He didn't believe they were there at all. He didn't believe they were capable of such a thing. If there was one man who was less likely to assault a policeman than Otto the Sausage, it was Rabbit Butler. The Bench reminded him that both these innocents had actually been discovered in Officer Keating's grasp. Mr. Buffin smiled a harassed smile, and wiped a drop of perspiration from his brow.

Officer Keating was enthusiastic. He described the affair from start to finish. But for Mr. Buffin he would have been killed. But for Mr. Buffin there would have been no prisoners in court that day. The world was full of men with more or less golden hearts, but there was only one Mr. Buffin. Might he shake hands with Mr. Buffin?

The magistrate ruled that he might. More, he would shake hands with him himself. Summoning Mr. Buffin behind his desk, he proceeded to do so. If there were more men like Mr. Buffin, London would be a better place. It was the occasional discovery in our midst of ethereal natures like that of Mr. Buffin which made one so confident for the future of the race.

The paragon shuffled out. It was bright and sunny in the street, but in Mr. Buffin's heart there was no sunlight. He was not a quick thinker, but he had come quite swiftly to the conclusion that London was no longer the place for him. Sid Marks had been in court chewing a straw and listening with grave attention to the evidence, and for one moment Mr. Buffin had happened to catch his eye. No medical testimony as to the unhealthiness of London could have moved him more.

Once round the corner, he ran. It hurt his head to run, but there were things behind him that could hurt his head more than running.

At the entrance to the Tube he stopped. To leave the locality he must have money. He felt in his pockets. Slowly, one by one, he pulled forth his little valuables. His knife ... his revolver ... the magistrate's gold watch ... He inspected them sadly. They must all go.

He went into a pawnbroker's shop at the corner of the street. A few moments later, with money in his pockets, he dived into the Tube.

The Best Sauce

Eve Hendrie sat up in bed. For two hours she had been trying to get to sleep, but without success. Never in her life had she felt more wakeful.

There were two reasons for this. Her mind was disturbed, and she was very hungry. Neither sensation was novel to her. Since first she had become paid companion to Mrs. Rastall-Retford there had hardly been a moment when she had not been hungry. Some time before Mrs. Rastall-Retford's doctor had recommended to that lady a Spartan diet, and in this Eve, as companion, had unwillingly to share. It was not pleasant for either of them, but at least Mrs. Rastall-Retford had the knowledge that she had earned it by years of honest self-indulgence. Eve had not that consolation.

Meagre fare, moreover, had the effect of accentuating Mrs. Rastall-Retford's always rather pronounced irritability. She was a massive lady, with a prominent forehead, some half-dozen chins, and a manner towards those in her employment which would have been resented in a second mate by the crew of a Western ocean tramp. Even at her best she was no ray of sunshine about the house. And since the beginning of the self-denying ordinance she had been at her worst.

But it was not depression induced by her employer that was disturbing Eve. That was a permanent evil. What was agitating her so extremely to-night was the unexpected arrival of Peter Rayner.

It was Eve's practice to tell herself several times a day that she had no sentiment for Peter Rayner but dislike. She did not attempt to defend her attitude logically, but nevertheless she clung to it, and to-night, when he entered the drawing-room, she had endeavoured to convey by her manner that it was only with the greatest difficulty that she remembered him at all, and that, having accomplished that feat, she now intended to forget him again immediately. And he had grinned a cheerful, affectionate grin, and beamed on her without a break till bedtime.

Before coming as companion to Mrs. Rastall-Retford Eve had been governess to Hildebrand, aged six, the son of a Mrs. Elphinstone. It had been, on the whole, a comfortable situation. She had not liked Mrs. Elphinstone, but Hildebrand had been docile, and altogether life was quite smooth and pleasant until Mrs. Elphinstone's brother came for a visit. Peter Rayner was that brother.

There is a type of man who makes love with the secrecy and sheepish reserve of a cowboy shooting up a Wild West saloon. To this class Peter belonged. He fell in love with Eve at sight, and if, at the end of the first day, there was anyone in the house who was not aware of it, it was only Hildebrand, aged six. And even Hildebrand must have had his suspicions.

Mrs. Elphinstone was among the first to become aware of it. For two days, frostily silent and gimlet-like as to the eye, she observed Peter's hurricane wooing from afar; then she acted. Peter she sent to London, pacifying him with an invitation to return to the house in the following week. This done, she proceeded to eliminate Eve. In the course of the parting interview she expressed herself perhaps a little less guardedly than was either just or considerate; and Eve, flushed and at war with the whole race of Rayners, departed that afternoon to seek a situation elsewhere. She had found it at the house of Mrs. Rastall-Retford.

And now this evening, as she sat in the drawing-room playing the piano to her employer, in had walked the latter's son, a tall, nervous young man, perpetually clearing his throat and fiddling with a pair of gold-rimmed glasses, with the announcement that he had brought his friend, Mr. Rayner, to spend a few days in the old home.

Eve could still see the look on Peter's face as, having shaken hands with his hostess, he turned to her. It was the look of the cowboy who, his weary ride over, sees through the dusk the friendly gleam of the saloon windows, and with a happy sigh reaches for his revolver. There could be no two meanings to that look. It said, as clearly as if he had shouted it, that this was no accidental meeting;

that he had tracked her down and proposed to resume matters at the point where they had left off.

Eve was indignant. It was abominable that he should pursue her in this way. She sat thinking how abominable it was for five minutes; and then it suddenly struck her that she was hungrier than ever. She had forgotten her material troubles for the moment. It seemed to her now that she was quite faint with hunger.

A cuckoo clock outside the door struck one. And, as it did so, it came to Eve that on the sideboard in the dining-room there were biscuits.

A moment later she was creeping softly down the stairs.

It was dark and ghostly on the stairs. The house was full of noises. She was glad when she reached the dining-room. It would be pleasant to switch on the light. She pushed open the door, and uttered a cry. The light was already switched on, and at the table, his back to her, was a man.

There was no time for flight. He must have heard the door open. In another moment he would turn and spring.

She spoke tremulously.

"Don't – don't move. I'm pointing a pistol at you."

The man did not move.

"Foolish child!" he said, indulgently. "Suppose it went off!"

She uttered an exclamation of surprise.

"You! What are you doing here, Mr. Rayner?"

She moved into the room, and her relief changed swiftly into indignation. On the table were half a chicken, a loaf, some cold potatoes, and a bottle of beer.

"I'm eating, thank goodness!" said Peter, helping himself to a cold potato. "I had begun to think I never should again."

"Eating!"

"Eating. I know a man of sensibility and refinement ought to shrink from raiding his hostess's larder in the small hours, but hunger's death to the finer feelings. It's the solar plexus punch which puts one's better self down and out for the count of ten. I am a large and healthy young man, and, believe me, I need this little snack. I need it badly. May I cut you a slice of chicken?"

She could hardly bear to look at it, but pride gave her strength.

"No," she snapped.

"You're sure? Poor little thing; I know you're half starved."

Eve stamped.

"How dare you speak to me like that, Mr. Rayner?"

He drank bottled beer thoughtfully.

"What made you come down? I suppose you heard a noise and thought it was burglars?" he said.

"Yes," said Eve, thankfully accepting the idea. At all costs she must conceal the biscuit motive.

"That was very plucky of you. Won't you sit down?"

"No, I'm going back to bed."

"Not just yet. I've several things to talk to you about. Sit down. That's right. Now cover up your poor little pink ankles, or you'll be catching—"

She started up.

"Mr. Rayner!"

"Sit down."

She looked at him defiantly, then, wondering at herself for doing it, sat down.

"Now," said Peter, "what do you mean by it? What do you mean by dashing off from my sister's house without leaving a word for me as to where you were going? You knew I loved you."

"Good night, Mr. Rayner."

"Sit down. You've given me a great deal of trouble. Do you know it cost me a sovereign in tips to find out your address? I couldn't get it out of my sister, and I had to apply to the butler. I've a good mind to knock it off your first week's pin-money."

"I shall not stay here listening—"

"You knew perfectly well I wanted to marry you. But you fly off without a word and bury yourself in this benighted place with a gorgon who nags and bullies you—"

"A nice way to speak of your hostess," said Eve, scornfully.

"A very soothing way. I don't think I ever took such a dislike to a woman at first sight before. And when she started to bullyrag you, it was all I could do – But it won't last long now. You must come away at once. We'll be married after Christmas, and in the meantime you can go and live with my sister—"

Eve listened speechlessly. She had so much to say that the difficulty of selection rendered her dumb.

"When can you start? I mean, do you have to give a month's notice or anything?"

Eve got up with a short laugh.

"Good night, Mr. Rayner," she said. "You have been very amusing, but I am getting tired."

"I'm glad it's all settled," said Peter. "Good night."

Eve stopped. She could not go tamely away without saying a single one of the things that crowded in her mind.

"Do you imagine," she said, "that I intend to marry you? Do you suppose, for one moment—"

"Rather!" said Peter. "You shall have a splendid time from now on, to make up for all you've gone through. I'm going to be awfully good to you, Eve. You sha'n't ever have any more worries, poor old thing." He looked at her affectionately. "I wonder why it is that large men always fall in love with little women. There are you, a fragile, fairy-like, ethereal wisp of a little creature; and here am I—"

"A great, big, greedy pig!" burst out Eve, "who thinks about nothing but eating and drinking."

"I wasn't going to have put it quite like that," said Peter, thoughtfully.

"I hate a greedy man," said Eve, between her teeth.

"I have a healthy appetite," protested Peter. "Nothing more. It runs in the family. At the time of the Civil War the Rayner of the period, who was King Charles's right-hand man, would frequently eat despatches to prevent them falling into the hands of the enemy. He was noted for it."

Eve reached the door and turned.

"I despise you," she said.

"Good night," said Peter, tenderly. "To-morrow morning we'll go for a walk."

His prediction proved absolutely correct. He was smoking a cigarette after breakfast when Eve came to him. Her face was pink and mutinous, but there was a gleam in her eye.

"Are you ready to come out, Mr. Rayner?" she said. "Mrs. Rastall-Retford says I'm to take you to see the view from the golf links."

"You'll like that," said Peter.

"I shall not like it," snapped Eve. "But Mrs. Rastall-Retford is paying me a salary to do what she tells me, and I have to earn it."

Conversation during the walk consisted mainly of a monologue on the part of Peter. It was a crisp and exhilarating morning, and he appeared to be feeling a universal benevolence towards all created things. He even softened slightly on the subject of Mrs. Rastall-Retford, and advanced the theory that her peculiar manner might be due to her having been ill-treated as a child.

Eve listened in silence. It was not till they were nearing home on their return journey that she spoke.

"Mr. Rayner," she said.

"Yes?" said Peter.

"I was talking to Mrs. Rastall-Retford after breakfast," said Eve, "and I told her something about you."

"My conscience is clear."

"Oh, nothing bad. Some people would say it was very much to your credit." She looked away across the fields. "I told her you were a vegetarian," she added, carelessly.

There was a long silence. Then Peter spoke three words, straight from the heart.

"You little devil!"

Eve turned and looked at him, her eyes sparkling wickedly.

"You see!" she said. "Now perhaps you will go."

"Without you?" said Peter, stoutly. "Never!"

"In London you will be able to eat all day – anything you like. You will be able to creep about your club gnawing cold chicken all night. But if you stay here—"

"You have got a wrong idea of the London clubman's life," said Peter. "If I crept about my club gnawing cold chicken I should have the committee after me. No, I shall stay here and look after you. After all, what is food?"

"I'll tell you what yours will be, if you like. Or would you rather wait and let it be a surprise? Well, for lunch you will have some boiled potatoes and cabbage and a sweet – a sort of light *souffle* thing. And for dinner—"

"Yes, but one moment," said Peter. "If I'm a vegetarian, how did you account for my taking all the chicken I could get at dinner last night, and looking as if I wanted more?"

"Oh, that was your considerateness. You didn't want to give trouble, even if you had to sacrifice your principles. But it's all right now. You are going to have your vegetables."

Peter drew a deep breath – the breath of the man who braces himself up and thanks whatever gods there be for his unconquerable soul.

"I don't care," he said. "A book of verses underneath the bough, a jug of wine, and thou—'"

"Oh, and I forgot," interrupted Eve. "I told her you were a tee-totaller as well."

There was another silence, longer than the first.

"The best train," said Eve, at last, "is the ten-fifty."

He looked at her inquiringly.

"The best train?"

"For London."

"What makes you think that I am interested in trains to London?"

Eve bit her lip.

"Mr. Rayner," she said, after a pause, "do you remember at lunch one day at Mrs. Elphinstone's refusing parsnips? You said that, so far as you were concerned, parsnips were first by a mile, and that prussic acid and strychnine also ran."

"Well?" said Peter.

"Oh, nothing," said Eve. "Only I made a stupid mistake. I told the cook you were devoted to parsnips. I'm sorry."

Peter looked at her gravely. "I'm putting up with a lot for your sake," he said.

"You needn't. Why don't you go away?"

"And leave you chained to the rock, Andromeda? Not for Perseus! I've only been here one night, but I've seen enough to know that I've got to take you away from this place. Honestly, it's killing you. I was watching you last night. You're scared if that infernal old woman starts to open her mouth. She's crushing the life out of you. I'm going to stay on here till you say you'll marry me, or till they throw me out."

"There are parsnips for dinner to-night," said Eve, softly.

"I shall get to like them. They are an acquired taste, I expect. Perhaps I am, too. Perhaps I am the human parsnip, and you will have to learn to love me."

"You are the human burr," said Eve, shortly. "I shouldn't have thought it possible for a man to behave as you are doing."

In spite of herself, there were moments during the next few days when Eve felt twinges of remorse. It was only by telling herself that he had no right to have followed her to this house, and that he was at perfect liberty to leave whenever he wished, that she could harden her heart again. And even this reflection was not entirely satisfactory, for it made her feel how fond he must be of her to endure these evils for her sake.

And there was no doubt about there being evils. It was a dreary house in which to spend winter days. There were no books that one could possibly read. The nearest railway station was five miles away. There was not even a dog to talk to. Generally it rained. Though Eve saw little of Peter, except at meals and in the drawing-room after dinner – for Mrs. Rastall-Retford spent most of the day in her own sitting-room and required Eve to be at her side – she could picture his sufferings, and, try as she would, she could not keep herself from softening a little. Her pride was weakening. Constant attendance on her employer was beginning to have a bad effect on her nerves. Association in a subordinate capacity with Mrs. Rastall-Retford did not encourage a proud and spirited outlook on life.

Her imagination had not exaggerated Peter's sufferings. Many people consider that Dante has spoken the last word on the post-mortem housing of the criminal classes. Peter, after the first week of his visit, could have given him a few new ideas.

It is unpleasant to be half starved. It is unpleasant to be cooped up in a country-house in winter with nothing to do. It is unpleasant to have to sit at meals and listen to the only girl you have ever really loved being bullyragged by an old lady with six chins. And all these unpleasantnesses were occurring to Peter simultaneously. It is highly creditable to him that the last should completely have outweighed the others.

He was generally alone. Mr. Rastall-Retford, who would have been better than nothing as a companion, was a man who enjoyed solitude. He was a confirmed vanisher. He would be present at one moment, the next he would have glided silently away. And, even on the rare occasions when he decided not to vanish, he seldom did much more than clear his throat nervously and juggle with his pince-nez.

Peter, in his boyhood, had been thrilled once by a narrative of a man who got stuck in the Sargasso Sea. It seemed to him now that the monotony of the Sargasso Sea had been greatly exaggerated.

Nemesis was certainly giving Peter his due. He had wormed his way into the Rastall-Retford home-circle by grossly deceitful means. The moment he heard that Eve had gone to live with Mrs. Rastall-Retford, and had ascertained that the Rastall-Retford with whom he had been at Cambridge and whom he still met occasionally at his club when he did not see him first, was this lady's son, he had set himself to court young Mr. Rastall-Retford. He had cornered him at the club and begun to talk about the dear old 'Varsity days, ignoring the embarrassment of the latter, whose only clear recollection of the dear old 'Varsity days as linking Peter and himself was of a certain bump-supper night, when sundry of the festive, led and inspired by Peter, had completely wrecked his rooms and shaved off half a growing moustache. He conveyed to young Mr. Rastall-Retford the impression that, in the dear old 'Varsity days, they had shared each other's joys and sorrows, and, generally, had made Damon and Pythias look like a pair of cross-talk knockabouts at one of the rowdier music-halls. Not to invite so old a friend to stay at his home, if he ever happened to be down that way, would, he hinted, be grossly churlish. Mr. Rastall-Retford, impressed, issued the invitation. And now Peter was being punished for his deceit. Nemesis may not be an Alfred Shrubb, but give her time and she gets there.

It was towards the middle of the second week of his visit that Eve, coming into the drawing-room before dinner, found Peter standing in front of the fire. They had not been alone together for several days.

"Well?" said he.

Eve went to the fire and warmed her hands.

"Well?" she said, dispiritedly.

She was feeling nervous and ill. Mrs. Rastall-Retford had been in one of her more truculent moods all day, and for the first time Eve had the sensation of being thoroughly beaten. She dreaded the long hours to bedtime. The thought that there might be bridge after dinner made her feel physically ill. She felt she could not struggle through a bridge night.

On the occasions when she was in one of her dangerous moods, Mrs. Rastall-Retford sometimes chose rest as a cure, sometimes relaxation. Rest meant that she retired to her room immediately after dinner, and expended her venom on her maid; relaxation meant bridge, and bridge seemed to bring out all her worst points. They played the game for counters at her house, and there had been occasions in Eve's experience when the loss of a hundred or so of these useful little adjuncts to Fun in the Home had lashed her almost into a frenzy. She was one of those bridge players who keep up a running quarrel with Fate during the game, and when she was not abusing Fate she was generally reproaching her partner. Eve was always her partner; and to-night she devoutly hoped that her employer would elect to rest. She always played badly with Mrs. Rastall-Retford, through sheer nervousness. Once she had revoked, and there had been a terrible moment and much subsequent recrimination.

Peter looked at her curiously.

"You're pale to-night," he said.

"I have a headache."

"H'm! How is our hostess? Fair? Or stormy?"

"As I was passing her door I heard her bullying her maid, so I suppose stormy."

"That means a bad time for you?" he said, sympathetically.

"I suppose so. If we play bridge. But she may go to bed directly after dinner."

She tried to keep her voice level, but he detected the break.

"Eve," he said, quickly, "won't you let me take you away from here? You've no business in this sort of game. You're not tough enough. You've got to be loved and made a fuss of and—"

She laughed shakily.

"Perhaps you can give me the address of some lady who wants a companion to love and make a fuss of?"

"I can give you the address of a man."

She rested an arm on the mantelpiece and stood looking into the blaze, without replying.

Before he could speak again there was a step outside the door, and Mrs. Rastall-Retford rustled into the room.

Eve had not misread the storm-signals. Her employer's mood was still as it had been earlier in the day. Dinner passed in almost complete silence. Mrs. Rastall-Retford sat brooding dumbly. Her eye was cold and menacing, and Peter, working his way through his vegetables, shuddered for Eve. He had understood her allusion to bridge, having been privileged several times during his stay to see his hostess play that game, and he hoped that there would be no bridge to-night.

And this was unselfish of him, for bridge meant sandwiches. Punctually at nine o'clock on bridge nights the butler would deposit on a side-table a plate of chicken sandwiches and (in deference to Peter's vegetarian views) a smaller plate of cheese sandwiches. At the close of play Mrs. Rastall-Retford would take one sandwich from each plate, drink a thimbleful of weak whisky and water, and retire.

Peter could always do with a sandwich or two these days. But he was prepared to abandon them joyfully if his hostess would waive bridge for this particular evening.

It was not to be. In the drawing-room Mrs. Rastall-Retford came out of her trance and called imperiously for the cards. Peter, when he saw his hand after the first deal, had a presentiment that if all his hands were to be as good as this, the evening was going to be a trying one. On the other occasions when they had played he had found it an extremely difficult task, even with moderate cards, to bring it about that his hostess should always win the odd rubber, for he was an excellent player, and, like most good players, had an artistic conscience which made it painful to him to play a deliberately bad game, even from the best motives. If all his hands were going to be as strong as this first one he saw that there was disaster ahead. He could not help winning.

Mrs. Rastall-Retford, who had dealt the first hand, made a most improper diamond declaration. Her son unfilially doubled, and, Eve having chicane – a tragedy which her partner evidently seemed to consider could have been avoided by the exercise of ordinary common sense – Peter and his partner, despite Peter's best efforts, won the game handsomely.

The son of the house dealt the next hand. Eve sorted her cards listlessly. She was feeling curiously tired. Her brain seemed dulled.

This hand, as the first had done, went all in favour of the two men. Mr. Rastall-Retford won five tricks in succession, and, judging from the glitter in his mild eye, was evidently going to win as many more as he possibly could. Mrs. Rastall-Retford glowered silently. There was electricity in the air.

The son of the house led a club. Eve played a card mechanically.

"Have you no clubs, Miss Hendrie?"

Eve started, and looked at her hand.

"No," she said.

Mrs. Rastall-Retford grunted suspiciously.

Not long ago, in Westport, Connecticut, U.S.A., a young man named Harold Sperry, a telephone worker, was boring a hole in the wall of a house with a view to passing a wire through it. He whistled joyously as he worked. He did not know that he had selected for purposes of perforation the exact spot where there lay, nestling in the brickwork, a large leaden water-pipe. The first intimation he had of that fact was when a jet of water suddenly knocked him fifteen feet into a rosebush.

As Harold felt then, so did Eve now, when, examining her hand once more to make certain that she had no clubs, she discovered the ace of that ilk peeping coyly out from behind the seven of spades.

Her face turned quite white. It is never pleasant to revoke at bridge, but to Eve just then it seemed a disaster beyond words. She looked across at her partner. Her imagination pictured the scene there would be ere long, unless—

It happens every now and then that the human brain shows in a crisis an unwonted flash of speed. Eve's did at this juncture. To her in her trouble there came a sudden idea.

She looked round the table. Mr. Rastall-Retford, having taken the last trick, had gathered it up in the introspective manner of one planning big *coups*, and was brooding tensely, with knit brows. His mother was frowning over her cards. She was unobserved.

She seized the opportunity. She rose from her seat, moved quickly to the side-table, and, turning her back, slipped the fatal card dexterously into the interior of a cheese sandwich.

Mrs. Rastall-Retford, absorbed, did not notice for an instant. Then she gave tongue.

"What are you doing, Miss Hendrie?"

Eve was breathing quickly.

"I – I thought that Mr. Rayner might like a sandwich."

She was at his elbow with the plate. It trembled in her hand.

"A sandwich! Kindly do not be so officious, Miss Hendrie. The idea – in the middle of a hand—" Her voice died away in a resentful mumble.

Peter started. He had been allowing his thoughts to wander. He looked from the sandwich to Eve and then at the sandwich again. He was puzzled. This had the aspect of being an olive-branch – could it be? Could she be meaning—? Or was it a subtle insult? Who could say? At any rate it was a sandwich, and he seized it, without prejudice.

"I hope at least you have had the sense to remember that Mr. Rayner is a vegetarian, Miss Hendrie," said Mrs. Rastall-Retford. "That is not a chicken sandwich?"

"No," said Eve; "it is not a chicken sandwich."

Peter beamed gratefully. He raised the olive-branch, and bit into it with the energy of a starving man. And as he did so he caught Eve's eye.

"Miss Hendrie!" cried Mrs. Rastall-Retford.

Eve started violently.

"Miss Hendrie, will you be good enough to play? The king of clubs to beat. I can't think what's the matter with you to-night."

"I'm very sorry," said Eve, and put down the nine of spades.

Mrs. Rastall-Retford glared.

"This is absurd," she cried. "You *must* have the ace of clubs. If you have not got it, who has? Look through your hand again. Is it there?"

"No."

"Then where can it be?"

"Where can it be?" echoed Peter, taking another bite.

"Why – why," said Eve, crimson, "I – I – have only five cards. I ought to have six."

"Five?" said Mrs. Rastall-Retford "Nonsense! Count again. Have you dropped it on the floor?"

Mr. Rastall-Retford stooped and looked under the table.

"It is not on the floor," he said. "I suppose it must have been missing from the pack before I dealt."

Mrs. Rastall-Retford threw down her cards and rose ponderously. It offended her vaguely that there seemed to be nobody to blame. "I shall go to bed," she said.

✽

Peter stood before the fire and surveyed Eve as she sat on the sofa. They were alone in the room, Mr. Rastall-Retford having drifted silently away in the wake of his mother. Suddenly Eve began to laugh helplessly.

He shook his head at her.

"This is considerably sharper than a serpent's tooth," he said. "You should be fawning gratefully upon me, not laughing. Do you suppose King Charles laughed at my ancestor when he ate the despatches? However, for the first time since I have been in this house I feel as if I had had a square meal."

Eve became suddenly serious. The smile left her face.

"Mr. Rayner, please don't think I'm ungrateful. I couldn't help laughing, but I can't tell you how grateful I am. You don't know what it would have been like if she had found out that I had revoked. I did it once before, and she kept on about it for days and days. It was awful." She shivered. "I think you must be right, and my nerves *are* going."

He nodded.

"So are you – to-morrow, by the first train. I wonder how soon we can get married. Do you know anything about special licenses?"

She looked at him curiously.

"You're very obstinate," she said.

"Firm," he corrected. "Firm. Could you pack to-night, do you think, and be ready for that ten-fifty to-morrow morning?"

She began to trace an intricate pattern on the floor with the point of her shoe.

"I can't imagine why you are fond of me!" she said. "I've been very horrid to you."

"Nonsense. You've been all that's sweet and womanly."

"And I want to tell you why," she went on. "Your – your sister—"

"Ah, I thought as much!"

"She – she saw that you seemed to be getting fond of me, and she—"

"She would!"

"Said some rather horrid things that – hurt," said Eve, in a low voice.

Peter crossed over to where she sat and took her hand.

"Don't you worry about her," he said. "She's not a bad sort really, but about once every six months she needs a brotherly talking-to, or she gets above herself. One is about due during the next few days."

He stroke her hand.

"Fasting," he said, thoughtfully, "clears and stimulates the brain. I fancy I shall be able to think out some rather special things to say to her this time."

JEEVES AND THE CHUMP CYRIL

You know, the longer I live, the more clearly I see that half the trouble in this bally world is caused by the light-hearted and thoughtless way in which chappies dash off letters of introduction and hand them to other chappies to deliver to chappies of the third part. It's one of those things that make you wish you were living in the Stone Age. What I mean to say is, if a fellow in those days wanted to give anyone a letter of introduction, he had to spend a month or so carving it on a large-sized boulder, and the chances were that the other chappie got so sick of lugging the thing round in the hot sun that he dropped it after the first mile. But nowadays it's so easy to write letters of introduction that everybody does it without a second thought, with the result that some perfectly harmless cove like myself gets in the soup.

Mark you, all the above is what you might call the result of my riper experience. I don't mind admitting that in the first flush of the thing, so to speak, when Jeeves told me – this would be about three weeks after I'd landed in America – that a blighter called Cyril Bassington-Bassington had arrived and I found that he had brought a letter of introduction to me from Aunt Agatha ... where was I? Oh, yes ... I don't mind admitting, I was saying, that just at first I was rather bucked. You see, after the painful events which had resulted in my leaving England I hadn't expected to get any sort of letter from Aunt Agatha which would pass the censor, so to speak. And it was a pleasant surprise to open this one and find it almost civil. Chilly, perhaps, in parts, but on the whole quite tolerably polite. I looked on the thing as a hopeful sign. Sort of olive-branch, you know. Or do I mean orange blossom? What I'm getting at is that the fact that Aunt Agatha was writing to me without calling me names seemed, more or less, like a step in the direction of peace.

And I was all for peace, and that right speedily. I'm not saying a word against New York, mind you. I liked the place, and was having quite a ripe time there. But the fact remains that a fellow who's been used to London all his life does get a trifle homesick on a foreign strand, and I wanted to pop back to the cosy old flat in Berkeley Street – which could only be done when Aunt Agatha had simmered down and got over the Glossop episode. I know that London is a biggish city, but, believe me, it isn't half big enough for any fellow to live in with Aunt Agatha when she's after him with the old hatchet. And so I'm bound to say I looked on this chump Bassington-Bassington, when he arrived, more or less as a Dove of Peace, and was all for him.

He would seem from contemporary accounts to have blown in one morning at seven-forty-five, that being the ghastly sort of hour they shoot you off the liner in New York. He was given the respectful raspberry by Jeeves, and told to try again about three hours later, when there would be a sporting chance of my having sprung from my bed with a glad cry to welcome another day and all that sort of thing. Which was rather decent of Jeeves, by the way, for it so happened that there was a slight estrangement, a touch of coldness, a bit of a row in other words, between us at the moment because of some rather priceless purple socks which I was wearing against his wishes: and a lesser man might easily have snatched at the chance of getting back at me a bit by loosing Cyril into my bedchamber at a moment when I couldn't have stood a two-minutes' conversation with my dearest pal. For until I have had my early cup of tea and have brooded on life for a bit absolutely undisturbed, I'm not much of a lad for the merry chit-chat.

So Jeeves very sportingly shot Cyril out into the crisp morning air, and didn't let me know of his existence till he brought his card in with the Bohea.

"And what might all this be, Jeeves?" I said, giving the thing the glassy gaze.

"The gentleman has arrived from England, I understand, sir. He called to see you earlier in the day."

"Good Lord, Jeeves! You don't mean to say the day starts earlier than this?"

"He desired me to say he would return later, sir."

"I've never heard of him. Have you ever heard of him, Jeeves?"

"I am familiar with the name Bassington-Bassington, sir. There are three branches of the Bassington-Bassington family – the Shropshire Bassington-Bassingtons, the Hampshire Bassington-Bassingtons, and the Kent Bassington-Bassingtons."

"England seems pretty well stocked up with Bassington-Bassingtons."

"Tolerably so, sir."

"No chance of a sudden shortage, I mean, what?"

"Presumably not, sir."

"And what sort of a specimen is this one?"

"I could not say, sir, on such short acquaintance."

"Will you give me a sporting two to one, Jeeves, judging from what you have seen of him, that this chappie is not a blighter or an excrescence?"

"No, sir. I should not care to venture such liberal odds."

"I knew it. Well, the only thing that remains to be discovered is what kind of a blighter he is."

"Time will tell, sir. The gentleman brought a letter for you, sir."

"Oh, he did, did he?" I said, and grasped the communication. And then I recognised the handwriting. "I say, Jeeves, this is from my Aunt Agatha!"

"Indeed, sir?"

"Don't dismiss it in that light way. Don't you see what this means? She says she wants me to look after this excrescence while he's in New York. By Jove, Jeeves, if I only fawn on him a bit, so that he sends back a favourable report to head-quarters, I may yet be able to get back to England in time for Goodwood. Now is certainly the time for all good men to come to the aid of the party, Jeeves. We must rally round and cosset this cove in no uncertain manner."

"Yes, sir."

"He isn't going to stay in New York long," I said, taking another look at the letter. "He's headed for Washington. Going to give the nibs there the once-over, apparently, before taking a whirl at the Diplomatic Service. I should say that we can win this lad's esteem and affection with a lunch and a couple of dinners, what?"

"I fancy that should be entirely adequate, sir."

"This is the jolliest thing that's happened since we left England. It looks to me as if the sun were breaking through the clouds."

"Very possibly, sir."

He started to put out my things, and there was an awkward sort of silence.

"Not those socks, Jeeves," I said, gulping a bit but having a dash at the careless, off-hand tone. "Give me the purple ones."

"I beg your pardon, sir?"

"Those jolly purple ones."

"Very good, sir."

He lugged them out of the drawer as if he were a vegetarian fishing a caterpillar out of the salad. You could see he was feeling deeply. Deuced painful and all that, this sort of thing, but a chappie has got to assert himself every now and then. Absolutely.

I was looking for Cyril to show up again any time after breakfast, but he didn't appear: so towards one o'clock I trickled out to the Lambs Club, where I had an appointment to feed the Wooster face with a cove of the name of Caffyn I'd got pally with since my arrival – George Caffyn, a fellow who wrote plays and what not. I'd made a lot of friends during my stay in New York, the city being crammed with bonhomous lads who one and all extended a welcoming hand to the stranger in their midst.

Caffyn was a bit late, but bobbed up finally, saying that he had been kept at a rehearsal of his new musical comedy, "Ask Dad"; and we started in. We had just reached the coffee, when the waiter came up and said that Jeeves wanted to see me.

Jeeves was in the waiting-room. He gave the socks one pained look as I came in, then averted his eyes.

"Mr. Bassington-Bassington has just telephoned, sir."

"Oh?"

"Yes, sir."

"Where is he?"

"In prison, sir."

I reeled against the wallpaper. A nice thing to happen to Aunt Agatha's nominee on his first morning under my wing, I did *not* think!

"In prison!"

"Yes, sir. He said on the telephone that he had been arrested and would be glad if you could step round and bail him out."

"Arrested! What for?"

"He did not favour me with his confidence in that respect, sir."

"This is a bit thick, Jeeves."

"Precisely, sir."

I collected old George, who very decently volunteered to stagger along with me, and we hopped into a taxi. We sat around at the police-station for a bit on a wooden bench in a sort of ante-room, and presently a policeman appeared, leading in Cyril.

"Halloa! Halloa! Halloa!" I said. "What?"

My experience is that a fellow never really looks his best just after he's come out of a cell. When I was up at Oxford, I used to have a regular job bailing out a pal of mine who never failed to get pinched every Boat-Race night, and he always looked like something that had been dug up by the roots. Cyril was in pretty much the same sort of shape. He had a black eye and a torn collar, and altogether was nothing to write home about – especially if one was writing to Aunt Agatha. He was a thin, tall chappie with a lot of light hair and pale-blue goggly eyes which made him look like one of the rarer kinds of fish.

"I got your message," I said.

"Oh, are you Bertie Wooster?"

"Absolutely. And this is my pal George Caffyn. Writes plays and what not, don't you know."

We all shook hands, and the policeman, having retrieved a piece of chewing-gum from the underside of a chair, where he had parked it against a rainy day, went off into a corner and began to contemplate the infinite.

"This is a rotten country," said Cyril.

"Oh, I don't know, you know, don't you know!" I said.

"We do our best," said George.

"Old George is an American," I explained. "Writes plays, don't you know, and what not."

"Of course, I didn't invent the country," said George. "That was Columbus. But I shall be delighted to consider any improvements you may suggest and lay them before the proper authorities."

"Well, why don't the policemen in New York dress properly?"

George took a look at the chewing officer across the room.

"I don't see anything missing," he said

"I mean to say, why don't they wear helmets like they do in London? Why do they look like postmen? It isn't fair on a fellow. Makes it dashed confusing. I was simply standing on the pavement, looking at things, when a fellow who looked like a postman prodded me in the ribs with a club. I didn't see why I should have postmen prodding me. Why the dickens should a fellow come three thousand miles to be prodded by postmen?"

"The point is well taken," said George. "What did you do?"

"I gave him a shove, you know. I've got a frightfully hasty temper, you know. All the Bassington-Bassingtons have got frightfully hasty tempers, don't you know! And then he biffed me in the eye and lugged me off to this beastly place."

"I'll fix it, old son," I said. And I hauled out the bank-roll and went off to open negotiations, leaving Cyril to talk to George. I don't mind admitting that I was a bit perturbed. There were furrows in the old brow, and I had a kind of foreboding feeling. As long as this chump stayed in New York, I was responsible for him: and he didn't give me the impression of being the species of cove a reasonable chappie would care to be responsible for for more than about three minutes.

I mused with a considerable amount of tensity over Cyril that night, when I had got home and Jeeves had brought me the final whisky. I couldn't help feeling that this visit of his to America was going to be one of those times that try men's souls and what not. I hauled out Aunt Agatha's letter of introduction and re-read it, and there was no getting away from the fact that she undoubtedly appeared to be somewhat wrapped up in this blighter and to consider it my mission in life to shield him from harm while on the premises. I was deuced thankful that he had taken such a liking for George Caffyn, old George being a steady sort of cove. After I had got him out of his dungeon-cell, he and old George had gone off together, as chummy as brothers, to watch the afternoon rehearsal of "Ask Dad." There was some talk, I gathered, of their dining together. I felt pretty easy in my mind while George had his eye on him.

I had got about as far as this in my meditations, when Jeeves came in with a telegram. At least, it wasn't a telegram: it was a cable – from Aunt Agatha – and this is what it said:—

Has Cyril Bassington-Bassington called yet? On no account intro-duce him into theatrical circles. Vitally important. Letter follows.

I read it a couple of times.

"This is rummy, Jeeves!"

"Yes, sir."

"Very rummy and dashed disturbing!"

"Will there be anything further to-night, sir?"

Of course, if he was going to be as bally unsympathetic as that there was nothing to be done. My idea had been to show him the cable and ask his advice. But if he was letting those purple socks rankle to that extent, the good old *noblesse oblige* of the Woosters couldn't lower itself to the extent of pleading with the man. Absolutely not. So I gave it a miss.

"Nothing more, thanks."

"Good night, sir."

"Good night."

He floated away, and I sat down to think the thing over. I had been directing the best efforts of the old bean to the problem for a matter of half an hour, when there was a ring at the bell. I went to the door, and there was Cyril, looking pretty festive.

"I'll come in for a bit if I may," he said. "Got something rather priceless to tell you."

He curveted past me into the sitting-room, and when I got there after shutting the front door I found him reading Aunt Agatha's cable and giggling in a rummy sort of manner. "Oughtn't to have looked at this, I suppose. Caught sight of my name and read it with-out thinking. I say, Wooster, old friend of my youth, this is rather funny. Do you mind if I have a drink? Thanks awfully and all that sort of rot. Yes, it's rather funny, considering what I came to tell you. Jolly old Caffyn has given me a small part in that musical comedy of his, 'Ask Dad.' Only a bit, you know, but quite tolerably ripe. I'm feeling frightfully braced, don't you know!"

He drank his drink, and went on. He didn't seem to notice that I wasn't jumping about the room, yapping with joy.

"You know, I've always wanted to go on the stage, you know," he said. "But my jolly old guv'nor wouldn't stick it at any price. Put the old Waukeesi down with a bang, and turned bright purple whenever the subject was mentioned. That's the real reason why I came over here, if you want to know. I knew there wasn't a chance of my being able to work this stage wheeze in London without somebody getting on to it and tipping off the guv'nor, so I rather brainily sprang the scheme of popping over to Washington to broaden my mind. There's nobody to interfere on this side, you see, so I can go right ahead!"

I tried to reason with the poor chump.

"But your guv'nor will have to know some time."

"That'll be all right. I shall be the jolly old star by then, and he won't have a leg to stand on."

"It seems to me he'll have one leg to stand on while he kicks me with the other."

"Why, where do you come in? What have you got to do with it?"

"I introduced you to George Caffyn."

"So you did, old top, so you did. I'd quite forgotten. I ought to have thanked you before. Well, so long. There's an early rehearsal of 'Ask Dad' to-morrow morning, and I must be toddling. Rummy the thing should be called 'Ask Dad,' when that's just what I'm not going to do. See what I mean, what, what? Well, pip-pip!"

"Toodle-oo!" I said sadly, and the blighter scudded off. I dived for the phone and called up George Caffyn.

"I say, George, what's all this about Cyril Bassington-Bassington?"

"What about him?"

"He tells me you've given him a part in your show."

"Oh, yes. Just a few lines."

"But I've just had fifty-seven cables from home telling me on no account to let him go on the stage."

"I'm sorry. But Cyril is just the type I need for that part. He's simply got to be himself."

"It's pretty tough on me, George, old man. My Aunt Agatha sent this blighter over with a letter of introduction to me, and she will hold me responsible."

"She'll cut you out of her will?"

"It isn't a question of money. But – of course, you've never met my Aunt Agatha, so it's rather hard to explain. But she's a sort of human vampire-bat, and she'll make things most fearfully unpleasant for me when I go back to England. She's the kind of woman who comes and rags you before breakfast, don't you know."

"Well, don't go back to England, then. Stick here and become President."

"But, George, old top—!"

"Good night!"

"But, I say, George, old man!"

"You didn't get my last remark. It was 'Good night!' You Idle Rich may not need any sleep, but I've got to be bright and fresh in the morning. God bless you!"

I felt as if I hadn't a friend in the world. I was so jolly well worked up that I went and banged on Jeeves's door. It wasn't a thing I'd have cared to do as a rule, but it seemed to me that now was the time for all good men to come to the aid of the party, so to speak, and that it was up to Jeeves to rally round the young master, even if it broke up his beauty-sleep.

Jeeves emerged in a brown dressing-gown.

"Sir?"

"Deuced sorry to wake you up, Jeeves, and what not, but all sorts of dashed disturbing things have been happening."

"I was not asleep. It is my practice, on retiring, to read a few pages of some instructive book."

"That's good! What I mean to say is, if you've just finished exercising the old bean, it's probably in mid-season form for tackling problems. Jeeves, Mr. Bassington-Bassington is going on the stage!"

"Indeed, sir?"

"Ah! The thing doesn't hit you! You don't get it properly! Here's the point. All his family are most fearfully dead against his going on the stage. There's going to be no end of trouble if he isn't headed off. And, what's worse, my Aunt Agatha will blame me, you see."

"I see, sir."

"Well, can't you think of some way of stopping him?"

"Not, I confess, at the moment, sir."

"Well, have a stab at it."

"I will give the matter my best consideration, sir. Will there be anything further to-night?"

"I hope not! I've had all I can stand already."

"Very good, sir."

He popped off.

The part which old George had written for the chump Cyril took up about two pages of typescript; but it might have been Hamlet, the way that poor, misguided pinhead worked himself to the bone over it. I suppose, if I heard him his lines once, I did it a dozen times in the first couple of days. He seemed to think that my only feeling about the whole affair was one of enthusiastic admiration, and that he could rely on my support and sympathy. What with trying to imagine how Aunt Agatha was going to take this thing, and being woken up out of the dreamless in the small hours every other night to give my opinion of some new bit of business which Cyril had invented, I became more or less the good old shadow. And all the time Jeeves remained still pretty cold and distant about the purple socks. It's this sort of thing that ages a chappie, don't you know, and makes his youthful *joie-de-vivre* go a bit groggy at the knees.

In the middle of it Aunt Agatha's letter arrived. It took her about six pages to do justice to Cyril's father's feelings in regard to his going on the stage and about six more to give me a kind of sketch of what she would say, think, and do if I didn't keep him clear of injurious influences while he was in America. The letter came by the afternoon mail, and left me with a pretty firm conviction that it wasn't a thing I ought to keep to myself. I didn't even wait to ring the bell: I whizzed for the kitchen, bleating for Jeeves, and butted into the middle of a regular tea-party of sorts. Seated at the table were a depressed-looking cove who might have been a valet or something, and a boy in a Norfolk suit. The valet-chappie was drinking a whisky and soda, and the boy was being tolerably rough with some jam and cake.

"Oh, I say, Jeeves!" I said. "Sorry to interrupt the feast of reason and flow of soul and so forth, but—"

At this juncture the small boy's eye hit me like a bullet and stopped me in my tracks. It was one of those cold, clammy, accusing sort of eyes – the kind that makes you reach up to see if your tie is straight: and he looked at me as if I were some sort of unnecessary product which Cuthbert the Cat had brought in after a ramble among the local ash-cans. He was a stoutish infant with a lot of freckles and a good deal of jam on his face.

"Hallo! Hallo! Hallo!" I said. "What?" There didn't seem much else to say.

The stripling stared at me in a nasty sort of way through the jam. He may have loved me at first sight, but the impression he gave me was that he didn't think a lot of me and wasn't betting much that I would improve a great deal on acquaintance. I had a kind of feeling that I was about as popular with him as a cold Welsh rabbit.

"What's your name?" he asked.

"My name? Oh, Wooster, don't you know, and what not."

"My pop's richer than you are!"

That seemed to be all about me. The child having said his say, started in on the jam again. I turned to Jeeves.

"I say, Jeeves, can you spare a moment? I want to show you something."

"Very good, sir." We toddled into the sitting-room.

"Who is your little friend, Sidney the Sunbeam, Jeeves?"

"The young gentleman, sir?"

"It's a loose way of describing him, but I know what you mean."

"I trust I was not taking a liberty in entertaining him, sir?"

"Not a bit. If that's your idea of a large afternoon, go ahead."

"I happened to meet the young gentleman taking a walk with his father's valet, sir, whom I used to know somewhat intimately in London, and I ventured to invite them both to join me here."

"Well, never mind about him, Jeeves. Read this letter."

He gave it the up-and-down.

"Very disturbing, sir!" was all he could find to say.

"What are we going to do about it?"

"Time may provide a solution, sir."

"On the other hand, it mayn't, what?"

"Extremely true, sir.".

We'd got as far as this, when there was a ring at the door. Jeeves shimmered off, and Cyril blew in, full of good cheer and blitheringness.

"I say, Wooster, old thing," he said, "I want your advice. You know this jolly old part of mine. How ought I to dress it? What I mean is, the first act scene is laid in an hotel of sorts, at about three in the afternoon. What ought I to wear, do you think?"

I wasn't feeling fit for a discussion of gent's suitings.

"You'd better consult Jeeves," I said.

"A hot and by no means unripe idea! Where is he?"

"Gone back to the kitchen, I suppose."

"I'll smite the good old bell, shall I? Yes? No?"

"Right-o!"

Jeeves poured silently in.

"Oh, I say, Jeeves," began Cyril, "I just wanted to have a syllable or two with you. It's this way – Hallo, who's this?"

I then perceived that the stout stripling had trickled into the room after Jeeves. He was standing near the door looking at Cyril as if his worst fears had been realised. There was a bit of a silence. The child remained there, drinking Cyril in for about half a minute; then he gave his verdict:

"Fish-face!"

"Eh? What?" said Cyril.

The child, who had evidently been taught at his mother's knee to speak the truth, made his meaning a trifle clearer.

"You've a face like a fish!"

He spoke as if Cyril was more to be pitied than censured, which I am bound to say I thought rather decent and broad-minded of him. I don't mind admitting that, whenever I looked at Cyril's face, I always had a feeling that he couldn't have got that way without its being mostly his own fault. I found myself warming to this child. Absolutely, don't you know. I liked his conversation.

It seemed to take Cyril a moment or two really to grasp the thing, and then you could hear the blood of the Bassington-Bassingtons begin to sizzle.

"Well, I'm dashed!" he said. "I'm dashed if I'm not!"

"I wouldn't have a face like that," proceeded the child, with a good deal of earnestness, "not if you gave me a million dollars." He thought for a moment, then corrected himself. "Two million dollars!" he added.

Just what occurred then I couldn't exactly say, but the next few minutes were a bit exciting. I take it that Cyril must have made a dive for the infant. Anyway, the air seemed pretty well congested with arms and legs and things. Something bumped into the Wooster waistcoat just around the third button, and I collapsed on to the settee and rather lost interest in things for the moment. When I had unscrambled myself, I found that Jeeves and the child had retired and Cyril was standing in the middle of the room snorting a bit.

"Who's that frightful little brute, Wooster?"

"I don't know. I never saw him before to-day."

"I gave him a couple of tolerably juicy buffets before he legged it. I say, Wooster, that kid said a dashed odd thing. He yelled out something about Jeeves promising him a dollar if he called me – er – what he said."

It sounded pretty unlikely to me.

"What would Jeeves do that for?"

"It struck me as rummy, too."

"Where would be the sense of it?"

"That's what I can't see."

"I mean to say, it's nothing to Jeeves what sort of a face you have!"

"No!" said Cyril. He spoke a little coldly, I fancied. I don't know why. "Well, I'll be popping. Toodle-oo!"

"Pip-pip!"

It must have been about a week after this rummy little episode that George Caffyn called me up and asked me if I would care to go and see a run-through of his show. "Ask Dad," it seemed, was to open out of town in Schenectady on the following Monday, and this was to be a sort of preliminary dress-rehearsal. A preliminary dress-rehearsal, old George explained, was the same as a regular dress-rehearsal inasmuch as it was apt to look like nothing on earth and last into the small hours, but more exciting because they wouldn't be timing the piece and consequently all the blighters who on these occasions let their angry passions rise would have plenty of scope for interruptions, with the result that a pleasant time would be had by all.

The thing was billed to start at eight o'clock, so I rolled up at ten-fifteen, so as not to have too long to wait before they began. The dress-parade was still going on. George was on the stage, talking to a cove in shirt-sleeves and an absolutely round chappie with big spectacles and a practically hairless dome. I had seen George with the latter merchant once or twice at the club, and I knew that he was Blumenfield, the manager. I waved to George, and slid into a seat at the back of the house, so as to be out of the way when the fighting started. Presently George hopped down off the stage and came and joined me, and fairly soon after that the curtain went down. The chappie at the piano whacked out a well-meant bar or two, and the curtain went up again.

I can't quite recall what the plot of "Ask Dad" was about, but I do know that it seemed able to jog along all right without much help from Cyril. I was rather puzzled at first. What I mean is, through brooding on Cyril and hearing him in his part and listening to his views on what ought and what ought not to be done, I suppose I had got a sort of impression rooted in the old bean that he was pretty well the backbone of the show, and that the rest of the company didn't do much except go on and fill in when he happened to be off the stage. I sat there for nearly half an hour, waiting for him to make his entrance, until I suddenly discovered he had been on from the start. He was, in fact, the rummy-looking plug-ugly who was now leaning against a potted palm a couple of feet from the O.P. side, trying to appear intelligent while the heroine sang a song about Love being like something which for the moment has slipped my memory. After the second refrain he began to dance in company with a dozen other equally weird birds. A painful spectacle for one who could see a vision of Aunt Agatha reaching for the hatchet and old Bassington-Bassington senior putting on his strongest pair of hob-nailed boots. Absolutely!

The dance had just finished, and Cyril and his pals had shuffled off into the wings when a voice spoke from the darkness on my right.

"Pop!"

Old Blumenfield clapped his hands, and the hero, who had just been about to get the next line off his diaphragm, cheesed it. I peered into the shadows. Who should it be but Jeeves's little playmate with the freckles! He was now strolling down the aisle with his hands in his pockets as if the place belonged to him. An air of respectful attention seemed to pervade the building.

"Pop," said the stripling, "that number's no good." Old Blumenfield beamed over his shoulder.

"Don't you like it, darling?"

"It gives me a pain."

"You're dead right."

"You want something zippy there. Something with a bit of jazz to it!"

"Quite right, my boy. I'll make a note of it. All right. Go on!"

I turned to George, who was muttering to himself in rather an overwrought way.

"I say, George, old man, who the dickens is that kid?"

Old George groaned a bit hollowly, as if things were a trifle thick.

"I didn't know he had crawled in! It's Blumenfield's son. Now we're going to have a Hades of a time!"

"Does he always run things like this?"

"Always!"

"But why does old Blumenfield listen to him?"

"Nobody seems to know. It may be pure fatherly love, or he may regard him as a mascot. My own idea is that he thinks the kid has exactly the amount of intelligence of the average member of the audience, and that what makes a hit with him will please the general public. While, conversely, what he doesn't like will be too rotten for anyone. The kid is a pest, a wart, and a pot of poison, and should be strangled!"

The rehearsal went on. The hero got off his line. There was a slight outburst of frightfulness between the stage-manager and a Voice named Bill that came from somewhere near the roof, the subject under discussion being where the devil Bill's "ambers" were at that particular juncture. Then things went on again until the moment arrived for Cyril's big scene.

I was still a trifle hazy about the plot, but I had got on to the fact that Cyril was some sort of an English peer who had come over to America doubtless for the best reasons. So far he had only had two lines to say. One was "Oh, I say!" and the other was "Yes, by Jove!"; but I seemed to recollect, from hearing him read his part, that pretty soon he was due rather to spread himself. I sat back in my chair and waited for him to bob up.

He bobbed up about five minutes later. Things had got a bit stormy by that time. The Voice and the stage-director had had another of their love-feasts – this time something to do with why Bill's "blues" weren't on the job or something. And, almost as soon as that was over, there was a bit of unpleasantness because a flower-pot fell off a window-ledge and nearly brained the hero. The atmosphere was consequently more or less hotted up when Cyril, who had been hanging about at the back of the stage, breezed down centre and toed the mark for his most substantial chunk of entertainment. The heroine had been saying something – I forget what – and all the chorus, with Cyril at their head, had begun to surge round her in the restless sort of way those chappies always do when there's a number coming along.

Cyril's first line was, "Oh, I say, you know, you mustn't say that, really!" and it seemed to me he passed it over the larynx with a good-ish deal of vim and *je-ne-sais-quoi*. But, by Jove, before the heroine had time for the come-back, our little friend with the freckles had risen to lodge a protest.

"Pop!"

"Yes, darling?"

"That one's no good!"

"Which one, darling?"

"The one with a face like a fish."

"But they all have faces like fish, darling."

The child seemed to see the justice of this objection. He became more definite.

"The ugly one."

"Which ugly one? That one?" said old Blumenfield, pointing to Cyril.

"Yep! He's rotten!"

"I thought so myself."

"He's a pill!"

"You're dead right, my boy. I've noticed it for some time."

Cyril had been gaping a bit while these few remarks were in progress. He now shot down to the footlights. Even from where I was sitting, I could see that these harsh words had hit the old Bassington-Bassington family pride a frightful wallop. He started to get pink in the ears, and then in the nose, and then in the cheeks, till in about a quarter of a minute he looked pretty much like an explosion in a tomato cannery on a sunset evening.

"What the deuce do you mean?"

"What the deuce do you mean?" shouted old Blumenfield. "Don't yell at me across the footlights!"

"I've a dashed good mind to come down and spank that little brute!"

"What!"

"A dashed good mind!"

Old Blumenfield swelled like a pumped-up tyre. He got rounder than ever.

"See here, mister – I don't know your darn name—!"

"My name's Bassington-Bassington, and the jolly old Bassington-Bassingtons – I mean the Bassington-Bassingtons aren't accustomed—"

Old Blumenfield told him in a few brief words pretty much what he thought of the Bassington-Bassingtons and what they weren't accustomed to. The whole strength of the company rallied round to enjoy his remarks. You could see them jutting out from the wings and protruding from behind trees.

"You got to work good for my pop!" said the stout child, waggling his head reprovingly at Cyril.

"I don't want any bally cheek from you!" said Cyril, gurgling a bit.

"What's that?" barked old Blumenfield. "Do you understand that this boy is my son?"

"Yes, I do," said Cyril. "And you both have my sympathy!"

"You're fired!" bellowed old Blumenfield, swelling a good bit more. "Get out of my theatre!"

About half-past ten next morning, just after I had finished lubricating the good old interior with a soothing cup of Oolong, Jeeves filtered into my bedroom, and said that Cyril was waiting to see me in the sitting-room.

"How does he look, Jeeves?"

"Sir?"

"What does Mr. Bassington-Bassington look like?"

"It is hardly my place, sir, to criticise the facial peculiarities of your friends."

"I don't mean that. I mean, does he appear peeved and what not?"

"Not noticeably, sir. His manner is tranquil."

"That's rum!"

"Sir?"

"Nothing. Show him in, will you?"

I'm bound to say I had expected to see Cyril showing a few more traces of last night's battle. I was looking for a bit of the overwrought soul and the quivering ganglions, if you know what I mean. He seemed pretty ordinary and quite fairly cheerful.

"Hallo, Wooster, old thing!"

"Cheero!"

"I just looked in to say good-bye."

"Good-bye?"

"Yes. I'm off to Washington in an hour." He sat down on the bed. "You know, Wooster, old top," he went on, "I've been thinking it all over, and really it doesn't seem quite fair to the jolly old guv'nor, my going on the stage and so forth. What do you think?"

"I see what you mean."

"I mean to say, he sent me over here to broaden my jolly old mind and words to that effect, don't you know, and I can't help thinking it would be a bit of a jar for the old boy if I gave him the bird and went on the stage instead. I don't know if you understand me, but what I mean to say is, it's a sort of question of conscience."

"Can you leave the show without upsetting everything?"

"Oh, that's all right. I've explained everything to old Blumen-field, and he quite sees my position. Of course, he's sorry to lose me – said he didn't see how he could fill my place and all that sort of thing – but, after all, even if it does land him in a bit of a hole, I think I'm right in resigning my part, don't you?"

"Oh, absolutely."

"I thought you'd agree with me. Well, I ought to be shifting. Awfully glad to have seen something of you, and all that sort of rot. Pip-pip!"

"Toodle-oo!"

He sallied forth, having told all those bally lies with the clear, blue, pop-eyed gaze of a young child. I rang for Jeeves. You know, ever since last night I had been exercising the old bean to some extent, and a good deal of light had dawned upon me.

"Jeeves!"

"Sir?"

"Did you put that pie-faced infant up to bally-ragging Mr. Bassington-Bassington?"

"Sir?"

"Oh, you know what I mean. Did you tell him to get Mr. Bassington-Bassington sacked from the 'Ask Dad' company?"

"I would not take such a liberty, sir." He started to put out my clothes. "It is possible that young Master Blumenfield may have gathered from casual remarks of mine that I did not consider the stage altogether a suitable sphere for Mr. Bassington-Bassington."

"I say, Jeeves, you know, you're a bit of a marvel."

"I endeavour to give satisfaction, sir."

"And I'm frightfully obliged, if you know what I mean. Aunt Agatha would have had sixteen or seventeen fits if you hadn't headed him off."

"I fancy there might have been some little friction and unpleasantness, sir. I am laying out the blue suit with the thin red stripe, sir. I fancy the effect will be pleasing."

It's a rummy thing, but I had finished breakfast and gone out and got as far as the lift before I remembered what it was that I had meant to do to reward Jeeves for his really sporting behaviour in this matter of the chump Cyril. It cut me to the heart to do it, but I had decided to give him his way and let those purple socks pass out of my life. After all, there are times when a cove must make sacrifices. I was just going to nip back and break the glad news to him, when the lift came up, so I thought I would leave it till I got home.

The coloured chappie in charge of the lift looked at me, as I hopped in, with a good deal of quiet devotion and what not.

"I wish to thank yo', suh," he said, "for yo' kindness."

"Eh? What?"

"Misto' Jeeves done give me them purple socks, as you told him. Thank yo' very much, suh!"

I looked down. The blighter was a blaze of mauve from the ankle-bone southward. I don't know when I've seen anything so dressy.

"Oh, ah! Not at all! Right-o! Glad you like them!" I said.

Well, I mean to say, what? Absolutely!

Jeeves in the Springtime

"'Morning, Jeeves," I said.

"Good morning, sir," said Jeeves.

He put the good old cup of tea softly on the table by my bed, and I took a refreshing sip. Just right, as usual. Not too hot, not too sweet, not too weak, not too strong, not too much milk, and not a drop spilled in the saucer. A most amazing cove, Jeeves. So dashed competent in every respect. I've said it before, and I'll say it again. I mean to say, take just one small instance. Every other valet I've ever had used to barge into my room in the morning while I was still asleep, causing much misery; but Jeeves seems to know when I'm awake by a sort of telepathy. He always floats in with the cup exactly two minutes after I come to life. Makes a deuce of a lot of difference to a fellow's day.

"How's the weather, Jeeves?"

"Exceptionally clement, sir."

"Anything in the papers?"

"Some slight friction threatening in the Balkans, sir. Otherwise, nothing."

"I say, Jeeves, a man I met at the club last night told me to put my shirt on Privateer for the two o'clock race this afternoon. How about it?"

"I should not advocate it, sir. The stable is not sanguine."

That was enough for me. Jeeves knows. How, I couldn't say, but he knows. There was a time when I would laugh lightly, and go ahead, and lose my little all against his advice, but not now.

"Talking of shirts," I said, "have those mauve ones I ordered arrived yet?"

"Yes, sir. I sent them back."

"Sent them back?"

"Yes, sir. They would not have become you."

Well, I must say I'd thought fairly highly of those shirtings, but I bowed to superior knowledge. Weak? I don't know. Most fellows, no doubt, are all for having their valets confine their activities to creasing trousers and what not without trying to run the home; but it's different with Jeeves. Right from the first day he came to me, I have looked on him as a sort of guide, philosopher, and friend.

"Mr. Little rang up on the telephone a few moments ago, sir. I informed him that you were not yet awake."

"Did he leave a message?"

"No, sir. He mentioned that he had a matter of importance to discuss with you, but confided no details."

"Oh, well, I expect I shall be seeing him at the club."

"No doubt, sir."

I wasn't what you might call in a fever of impatience. Bingo Little is a chap I was at school with, and we see a lot of each other still. He's the nephew of old Mortimer Little, who retired from business recently with a goodish pile. (You've probably heard of Little's Liniment – It Limbers Up the Legs.) Bingo biffs about London on a pretty comfortable allowance given him by his uncle, and leads on the whole a fairly unclouded life. It wasn't likely that anything which he described as a matter of importance would turn out to be really so frightfully important. I took it that he had discovered some new brand of cigarette which he wanted me to try, or something like that, and didn't spoil my breakfast by worrying.

After breakfast I lit a cigarette and went to the open window to inspect the day. It certainly was one of the best and brightest.

"Jeeves," I said.

"Sir?" said Jeeves. He had been clearing away the breakfast things, but at the sound of the young master's voice cheesed it courteously.

"You were absolutely right about the weather. It is a juicy morning."

"Decidedly, sir."

"Spring and all that."

"Yes, sir."

"In the spring, Jeeves, a livelier iris gleams upon the burnished dove."

"So I have been informed, sir."

"Right ho! Then bring me my whangee, my yellowest shoes, and the old green Homburg. I'm going into the Park to do pastoral dances."

I don't know if you know that sort of feeling you get on these days round about the end of April and the beginning of May, when the sky's a light blue, with cotton-wool clouds, and there's a bit of a breeze blowing from the west? Kind of uplifted feeling. Romantic, if you know what I mean. I'm not much of a ladies' man, but on this particular morning it seemed to me that what I really wanted was some charming girl to buzz up and ask me to save her from assassins or something. So that it was a bit of an anti-climax when I merely ran into young Bingo Little, looking perfectly foul in a crimson satin tie decorated with horseshoes.

"Hallo, Bertie," said Bingo.

"My God, man!" I gargled. "The cravat! The gent's neckwear! Why? For what reason?"

"Oh, the tie?" He blushed. "I – er – I was given it."

He seemed embarrassed, so I dropped the subject. We toddled along a bit, and sat down on a couple of chairs by the Serpentine.

"Jeeves tells me you want to talk to me about something," I said.

"Eh?" said Bingo, with a start. "Oh yes, yes. Yes."

I waited for him to unleash the topic of the day, but he didn't seem to want to get going. Conversation languished. He stared straight ahead of him in a glassy sort of manner.

"I say, Bertie," he said, after a pause of about an hour and a quarter.

"Hallo!"

"Do you like the name Mabel?"

"No."

"No?"

"No."

"You don't think there's a kind of music in the word, like the wind rustling gently through the tree-tops?"

"No."

He seemed disappointed for a moment; then cheered up.

"Of course, you wouldn't. You always were a fatheaded worm without any soul, weren't you?"

"Just as you say. Who is she? Tell me all."

For I realised now that poor old Bingo was going through it once again. Ever since I have known him – and we were at school together – he has been perpetually falling in love with someone, generally in the spring, which seems to act on him like magic. At school he had the finest collection of actresses' photographs of anyone of his time; and at Oxford his romantic nature was a byword.

"You'd better come along and meet her at lunch," he said, looking at his watch.

"A ripe suggestion," I said. "Where are you meeting her? At the Ritz?"

"Near the Ritz."

He was geographically accurate. About fifty yards east of the Ritz there is one of those blighted tea-and-bun shops you see dotted about all over London, and into this, if you'll believe me, young Bingo dived like a homing rabbit; and before I had time to say a word we were wedged in at a table, on the brink of a silent pool of coffee left there by an early luncher.

I'm bound to say I couldn't quite follow the development of the scenario. Bingo, while not absolutely rolling in the stuff, has always had a fair amount of the ready. Apart from what he got from his uncle, I knew that he had finished up the jumping season well on the right side of the ledger. Why, then, was he lunching the girl at this God-forsaken eatery? It couldn't be because he was hard up.

Just then the waitress arrived. Rather a pretty girl.

"Aren't we going to wait—?" I started to say to Bingo, thinking it somewhat thick that, in addition to asking a girl to lunch with him in a place like this, he should fling himself on the foodstuffs before she turned up, when I caught sight of his face, and stopped.

The man was goggling. His entire map was suffused with a rich blush. He looked like the Soul's Awakening done in pink.

"Hallo, Mabel!" he said, with a sort of gulp.

"Hallo!" said the girl.

"Mabel," said Bingo, "this is Bertie Wooster, a pal of mine."

"Pleased to meet you," she said. "Nice morning."

"Fine," I said.

"You see I'm wearing the tie," said Bingo.

"It suits you beautiful," said the girl.

Personally, if anyone had told me that a tie like that suited me, I should have risen and struck them on the mazzard, regardless of their age and sex; but poor old Bingo simply got all flustered with gratification, and smirked in the most gruesome manner.

"Well, what's it going to be to-day?" asked the girl, introducing the business touch into the conversation.

Bingo studied the menu devoutly.

"I'll have a cup of cocoa, cold veal and ham pie, slice of fruit cake, and a macaroon. Same for you, Bertie?"

I gazed at the man, revolted. That he could have been a pal of mine all these years and think me capable of insulting the old turn with this sort of stuff cut me to the quick.

"Or how about a bit of hot steak-pudding, with a sparkling limado to wash it down?" said Bingo.

You know, the way love can change a fellow is really frightful to contemplate. This chappie before me, who spoke in that absolutely careless way of macaroons and limado, was the man I had seen in happier days telling the head-waiter at Claridge's exactly how he wanted the *chef* to prepare the *sole frite au gourmet aux champignons*, and saying he would jolly well sling it back if it wasn't just right. Ghastly! Ghastly!

A roll and butter and a small coffee seemed the only things on the list that hadn't been specially prepared by the nastier-minded members of the Borgia family for people they had a particular grudge against, so I chose them, and Mabel hopped it.

"Well?" said Bingo rapturously.

I took it that he wanted my opinion of the female poisoner who had just left us.

"Very nice," I said.

He seemed dissatisfied.

"You don't think she's the most wonderful girl you ever saw?" he said wistfully.

"Oh, absolutely!" I said, to appease the blighter. "Where did you meet her?"

"At a subscription dance at Camberwell."

"What on earth were you doing at a subscription dance at Camberwell?"

"Your man Jeeves asked me if I would buy a couple of tickets. It was in aid of some charity or other."

"Jeeves? I didn't know he went in for that sort of thing."

"Well, I suppose he has to relax a bit every now and then. Anyway, he was there, swinging a dashed efficient shoe. I hadn't meant to go at first, but I turned up for a lark. Oh, Bertie, think what I might have missed!"

"What might you have missed?" I asked, the old lemon being slightly clouded.

"Mabel, you chump. If I hadn't gone I shouldn't have met Mabel."

"Oh, ah!"

At this point Bingo fell into a species of trance, and only came out of it to wrap himself round the pie and macaroon.

"Bertie," he said, "I want your advice."

"Carry on."

"At least, not your advice, because that wouldn't be much good to anybody. I mean, you're a pretty consummate old ass, aren't you? Not that I want to hurt your feelings, of course."

"No, no, I see that."

"What I wish you would do is to put the whole thing to that fellow Jeeves of yours, and see what he suggests. You've often told me that he has helped other pals of yours out of messes. From what you tell me, he's by way of being the brains of the family."

"He's never let me down yet."

"Then put my case to him."

"What case?"

"My problem."

"What problem?"

"Why, you poor fish, my uncle, of course. What do you think my uncle's going to say to all this? If I sprang it on him cold, he'd tie himself in knots on the hearthrug."

"One of these emotional Johnnies, eh?"

"Somehow or other his mind has got to be prepared to receive the news. But how?"

"Ah!"

"That's a lot of help, that 'ah'! You see, I'm pretty well dependent on the old boy. If he cut off my allowance, I should be very much in the soup. So you put the whole binge to Jeeves and see if he can't scare up a happy ending somehow. Tell him my future is in his hands, and that, if the wedding bells ring out, he can rely on me, even unto half my kingdom. Well, call it ten quid. Jeeves would exert himself with ten quid on the horizon, what?"

"Undoubtedly," I said.

I wasn't in the least surprised at Bingo wanting to lug Jeeves into his private affairs like this. It was the first thing I would have thought of doing myself if I had been in any hole of any description. As I have frequently had occasion to observe, he is a bird of the ripest intellect, full of bright ideas. If anybody could fix things for poor old Bingo, he could.

I stated the case to him that night after dinner.

"Jeeves."

"Sir?"

"Are you busy just now?"

"No, sir."

"I mean, not doing anything in particular?"

"No, sir. It is my practice at this hour to read some improving book; but, if you desire my services, this can easily be postponed, or, indeed, abandoned altogether."

"Well, I want your advice. It's about Mr. Little."

"Young Mr. Little, sir, or the elder Mr. Little, his uncle, who lives in Pounceby Gardens?"

Jeeves seemed to know everything. Most amazing thing. I'd been pally with Bingo practically all my life, and yet I didn't remember ever having heard that his uncle lived anywhere in particular.

"How did you know he lived in Pounceby Gardens?" I said.

"I am on terms of some intimacy with the elder Mr. Little's cook, sir. In fact, there is an understanding."

I'm bound to say that this gave me a bit of a start. Somehow I'd never thought of Jeeves going in for that sort of thing.

"Do you mean you're engaged?"

"It may be said to amount to that, sir."

"Well, well!"

"She is a remarkably excellent cook, sir," said Jeeves, as though he felt called on to give some explanation. "What was it you wished to ask me about Mr. Little?"

I sprang the details on him.

"And that's how the matter stands, Jeeves," I said. "I think we ought to rally round a trifle and help poor old Bingo put the thing through. Tell me about old Mr. Little. What sort of a chap is he?"

"A somewhat curious character, sir. Since retiring from business he has become a great recluse, and now devotes himself almost entirely to the pleasures of the table."

"Greedy hog, you mean?"

"I would not, perhaps, take the liberty of describing him in precisely those terms, sir. He is what is usually called a gourmet. Very particular about what he eats, and for that reason sets a high value on Miss Watson's services."

"The cook?"

"Yes, sir."

"Well, it looks to me as though our best plan would be to shoot young Bingo in on him after dinner one night. Melting mood, I mean to say, and all that."

"The difficulty is, sir, that at the moment Mr. Little is on a diet, owing to an attack of gout."

"Things begin to look wobbly."

"No, sir, I fancy that the elder Mr. Little's misfortune may be turned to the younger Mr. Little's advantage. I was speaking only the other day to Mr. Little's valet, and he was telling me that it has become his principal duty to read to Mr. Little in the evenings. If I were in your place, sir, I should send young Mr. Little to read to his uncle."

"Nephew's devotion, you mean? Old man touched by kindly action, what?"

"Partly that, sir. But I would rely more on young Mr. Little's choice of literature."

"That's no good. Jolly old Bingo has a kind face, but when it comes to literature he stops at the *Sporting Times*."

"That difficulty may be overcome. I would be happy to select books for Mr. Little to read. Perhaps I might explain my idea further?"

"I can't say I quite grasp it yet."

"The method which I advocate is what, I believe, the advertisers call Direct Suggestion, sir, consisting as it does of driving an idea home by constant repetition. You may have had experience of the system?"

"You mean they keep on telling you that some soap or other is the best, and after a bit you come under the influence and charge round the corner and buy a cake?"

"Exactly, sir. The same method was the basis of all the most valuable propaganda during the recent war. I see no reason why it should not be adopted to bring about the desired result with regard to the subject's views on class distinctions. If young Mr. Little were to read day after day to his uncle a series of narratives in which marriage with young persons of an inferior social status was held up as both feasible and admirable, I fancy it would prepare the elder Mr. Little's mind for the reception of the information that his nephew wishes to marry a waitress in a tea-shop."

"*Are* there any books of that sort nowadays? The only ones I ever see mentioned in the papers are about married couples who find life grey, and can't stick each other at any price."

"Yes, sir, there are a great many, neglected by the reviewers but widely read. You have never encountered 'All for Love,' by Rosie M. Banks?"

"No."

"Nor 'A Red, Red Summer Rose,' by the same author?"

"No."

"I have an aunt, sir, who owns an almost complete set of Rosie M. Banks'. I could easily borrow as many volumes as young Mr. Little might require. They make very light, attractive reading."

"Well, it's worth trying."

"I should certainly recommend the scheme, sir."

"All right, then. Toddle round to your aunt's to-morrow and grab a couple of the fruitiest. We can but have a dash at it."

"Precisely, sir."

Bingo reported three days later that Rosie M. Banks was the goods and beyond a question the stuff to give the troops. Old Little had jibbed somewhat at first at the proposed change of literary diet, he not being much of a lad for fiction and having stuck hitherto exclusively to the heavier monthly reviews; but Bingo had got chapter one of "All for Love" past his guard before he knew what was happening, and after that there was nothing to it. Since then they had finished "A Red, Red Summer Rose," "Madcap Myrtle" and "Only a Factory Girl," and were halfway through "The Courtship of Lord Strathmorlick."

Bingo told me all this in a husky voice over an egg beaten up in sherry. The only blot on the thing from his point of view was that it wasn't doing a bit of good to the old vocal cords, which were beginning to show signs of cracking under the strain. He had been looking his symptoms up in a medical dictionary, and he thought he had got "clergyman's throat." But against this you had to set the fact that he was making an undoubted hit in the right quarter, and also that after the evening's reading he always stayed on to dinner; and, from what he told me, the dinners turned out by old Little's cook had to be tasted to be believed. There were tears in the old blighter's eyes as he got on the subject of the clear soup. I suppose to a fellow who for weeks had been tackling macaroons and limado it must have been like Heaven.

Old Little wasn't able to give any practical assistance at these banquets, but Bingo said that he came to the table and had his whack of arrowroot, and sniffed the dishes, and told stories of *entrees* he had had in the past, and sketched out scenarios of what he was going to do to the bill of fare in the future, when the doctor put him in shape; so I suppose he enjoyed himself, too, in a way. Anyhow, things seemed to be buzzing along quite satisfactorily, and Bingo said he had got an idea which, he thought, was going to clinch the thing. He wouldn't tell me what it was, but he said it was a pippin.

"We make progress, Jeeves," I said.

"That is very satisfactory, sir."

"Mr. Little tells me that when he came to the big scene in 'Only a Factory Girl,' his uncle gulped like a stricken bull-pup."

"Indeed, sir?"

"Where Lord Claude takes the girl in his arms, you know, and says—"

"I am familiar with the passage, sir. It is distinctly moving. It was a great favourite of my aunt's."

"I think we're on the right track."

"It would seem so, sir."

"In fact, this looks like being another of your successes. I've always said, and I always shall say, that for sheer brain, Jeeves, you stand alone. All the other great thinkers of the age are simply in the crowd, watching you go by."

"Thank you very much, sir. I endeavour to give satisfaction."

About a week after this, Bingo blew in with the news that his uncle's gout had ceased to trouble him, and that on the morrow he would be back at the old stand working away with knife and fork as before.

"And, by the way," said Bingo, "he wants you to lunch with him tomorrow."

"Me? Why me? He doesn't know I exist."

"Oh, yes, he does. I've told him about you."

"What have you told him?"

"Oh, various things. Anyhow, he wants to meet you. And take my tip, laddie – you go! I should think lunch to-morrow would be something special."

I don't know why it was, but even then it struck me that there was something dashed odd – almost sinister, if you know what I mean – about young Bingo's manner. The old egg had the air of one who has something up his sleeve.

"There is more in this than meets the eye," I said. "Why should your uncle ask a fellow to lunch whom he's never seen?"

"My dear old fathead, haven't I just said that I've been telling him all about you – that you're my best pal – at school together, and all that sort of thing?"

"But even then – and another thing. Why are you so dashed keen on my going?"

Bingo hesitated for a moment.

"Well, I told you I'd got an idea. This is it. I want you to spring the news on him. I haven't the nerve myself."

"What! I'm hanged if I do!"

"And you call yourself a pal of mine!"

"Yes, I know; but there are limits."

"Bertie," said Bingo reproachfully, "I saved your life once."

"When?"

"Didn't I? It must have been some other fellow, then. Well, anyway, we were boys together and all that. You can't let me down."

"Oh, all right," I said. "But, when you say you haven't nerve enough for any dashed thing in the world, you misjudge yourself. A fellow who—"

"Cheerio!" said young Bingo. "One-thirty to-morrow. Don't be late."

I'm bound to say that the more I contemplated the binge, the less I liked it. It was all very well for Bingo to say that I was slated for a magnificent lunch; but what good is the best possible lunch to a fellow if he is slung out into the street on his ear during the soup course? However, the word of a Wooster is his bond and all that sort of rot, so at one-thirty next day I tottered up the steps of No. 16, Pounceby Gardens, and punched the bell. And half a minute later I was up in the drawing-room, shaking hands with the fattest man I have ever seen in my life.

The motto of the Little family was evidently "variety." Young Bingo is long and thin and hasn't had a superfluous ounce on him since we first met; but the uncle restored the average and a bit over. The hand which grasped mine wrapped it round and enfolded it till I began to wonder if I'd ever get it out without excavating machinery.

"Mr. Wooster, I am gratified – I am proud – I am honoured."

It seemed to me that young Bingo must have boosted me to some purpose.

"Oh, ah!" I said.

He stepped back a bit, still hanging on to the good right hand.

"You are very young to have accomplished so much!"

I couldn't follow the train of thought. The family, especially my Aunt Agatha, who has savaged me incessantly from childhood up, have always rather made a point of the fact that mine is a wasted life, and that, since I won the prize at my first school for the best collection of wild flowers made during the summer holidays, I haven't done a dam' thing to land me on the nation's scroll of fame. I was wondering if he couldn't have got me mixed up with someone else, when the telephone-bell rang outside in the hall, and the maid came in to say that I was wanted. I buzzed down, and found it was young Bingo.

"Hallo!" said young Bingo. "So you've got there? Good man! I knew I could rely on you. I say, old crumpet, did my uncle seem pleased to see you?"

"Absolutely all over me. I can't make it out."

"Oh, that's all right. I just rang up to explain. The fact is, old man, I know you won't mind, but I told him that you were the author of those books I've been reading to him."

"What!"

"Yes, I said that 'Rosie M. Banks' was your pen-name, and you didn't want it generally known, because you were a modest, retiring sort of chap. He'll listen to you now. Absolutely hang on your words. A brightish idea, what? I doubt if Jeeves in person could have thought up a better one than that. Well, pitch it strong, old lad, and keep steadily before you the fact that I must have my allowance raised. I can't possibly marry on what I've got now. If this film is to end with the slow fade-out on the embrace, at least double is indicated. Well, that's that. Cheerio!"

And he rang off. At that moment the gong sounded, and the genial host came tumbling downstairs like the delivery of a ton of coals.

I always look back to that lunch with a sort of aching regret. It was the lunch of a lifetime, and I wasn't in a fit state to appreciate it. Subconsciously, if you know what I mean, I could see it was pretty special, but I had got the wind up to such a frightful extent over the ghastly situation in which young Bingo had landed me that its deeper meaning never really penetrated. Most of the time I might have been eating sawdust for all the good it did me.

Old Little struck the literary note right from the start.

"My nephew has probably told you that I have been making a close study of your books of late?" he began.

"Yes. He did mention it. How – er – how did you like the bally things?"

He gazed reverently at me.

"Mr. Wooster, I am not ashamed to say that the tears came into my eyes as I listened to them. It amazes me that a man as young as you can have been able to plumb human nature so surely to its depths; to play with so unerring a hand on the quivering heart-strings of your reader; to write novels so true, so human, so moving, so vital!"

"Oh, it's just a knack," I said.

The good old persp. was bedewing my forehead by this time in a pretty lavish manner. I don't know when I've been so rattled.

"Do you find the room a trifle warm?"

"Oh, no, no, rather not. Just right."

"Then it's the pepper. If my cook has a fault – which I am not prepared to admit – it is that she is inclined to stress the pepper a trifle in her made dishes. By the way, do you like her cooking?"

I was so relieved that we had got off the subject of my literary output that I shouted approval in a ringing baritone.

"I am delighted to hear it, Mr. Wooster. I may be prejudiced, but to my mind that woman is a genius."

"Absolutely!" I said.

"She has been with me seven years, and in all that time I have not known her guilty of a single lapse from the highest standard. Except once, in the winter of 1917, when a purist might have condemned a certain mayonnaise of hers as lacking in creaminess. But one must make allowances. There had been several air-raids about that time, and no doubt the poor woman was shaken. But nothing is perfect in this world, Mr. Wooster, and I have had my cross to bear. For seven years I have lived in constant apprehension lest some evilly-disposed person might lure her from my employment. To my certain knowledge she has received offers, lucrative offers, to accept service elsewhere. You may judge of my dismay, Mr. Wooster, when only this morning the bolt fell. She gave notice!"

"Good Lord!"

"Your consternation does credit, if I may say so, to the heart of the author of 'A Red, Red Summer Rose.' But I am thankful to say the worst has not happened. The matter has been adjusted. Jane is not leaving me."

"Good egg!"

"Good egg, indeed – though the expression is not familiar to me. I do not remember having come across it in your books. And, speaking of your books, may I say that what has impressed me about them even more than the moving poignancy of the actual narrative, is your philosophy of life. If there were more men like you, Mr. Wooster, London would be a better place."

This was dead opposite to my Aunt Agatha's philosophy of life, she having always rather given me to understand that it is the presence in it of chappies like me that makes London more or less of a plague spot; but I let it go.

"Let me tell you, Mr. Wooster, that I appreciate your splendid defiance of the outworn fetishes of a purblind social system. I appreciate it! You are big enough to see that rank is but the guinea stamp and that, in the magnificent words of Lord Bletchmore in 'Only a Factory Girl,' 'Be her origin ne'er so humble, a good woman is the equal of the finest lady on earth!'"

I sat up.

"I say! Do you think that?"

"I do, Mr. Wooster. I am ashamed to say that there was a time when I was like other men, a slave to the idiotic convention which we call Class Distinction. But, since I read your books—"

I might have known it. Jeeves had done it again.

"You think it's all right for a chappie in what you might call a certain social position to marry a girl of what you might describe as the lower classes?"

"Most assuredly I do, Mr. Wooster."

I took a deep breath, and slipped him the good news.

"Young Bingo – your nephew, you know – wants to marry a waitress," I said.

"I honour him for it," said old Little.

"You don't object?"

"On the contrary."

I took another deep breath and shifted to the sordid side of the business.

"I hope you won't think I'm butting in, don't you know," I said, "but – er – well, how about it?"

"I fear I do not quite follow you."

"Well, I mean to say, his allowance and all that. The money you're good enough to give him. He was rather hoping that you might see your way to jerking up the total a bit."

Old Little shook his head regretfully.

"I fear that can hardly be managed. You see, a man in my position is compelled to save every penny. I will gladly continue my nephew's existing allowance, but beyond that I cannot go. It would not be fair to my wife."

"What! But you're not married?"

"Not yet. But I propose to enter upon that holy state almost immediately. The lady who for years has cooked so well for me honoured me by accepting my hand this very morning." A cold gleam of triumph came into his eye. "Now let 'em try to get her away from me!" he muttered, defiantly.

"Young Mr. Little has been trying frequently during the after-noon to reach you on the telephone, sir," said Jeeves that night, when I got home.

"I'll bet he has," I said. I had sent poor old Bingo an outline of the situation by messenger-boy shortly after lunch.

"He seemed a trifle agitated."

"I don't wonder. Jeeves," I said, "so brace up and bite the bullet. I'm afraid I've bad news for you.

"That scheme of yours – reading those books to old Mr. Little and all that – has blown out a fuse."

"They did not soften him?"

"They did. That's the whole bally trouble. Jeeves, I'm sorry to say that *fiancee* of yours – Miss Watson, you know – the cook, you know – well, the long and the short of it is that she's chosen riches instead of honest worth, if you know what I mean."

"Sir?"

"She's handed you the mitten and gone and got engaged to old Mr. Little!"

"Indeed, sir?"

"You don't seem much upset."

"That fact is, sir, I had anticipated some such outcome."

I stared at him. "Then what on earth did you suggest the scheme for?"

"To tell you the truth, sir, I was not wholly averse from a sever-ance of my relations with Miss Watson. In fact, I greatly desired it. I respect Miss Watson exceedingly, but I have seen for a long time that we were not suited. Now, the *other* young person with whom I have an understanding—"

"Great Scott, Jeeves! There isn't another?"

"Yes, sir."

"How long has this been going on?"

"For some weeks, sir. I was greatly attracted by her when I first met her at a subscription dance at Camberwell."

"My sainted aunt! Not—"

Jeeves inclined his head gravely.

"Yes, sir. By an odd coincidence it is the same young person that young Mr. Little – I have placed the cigarettes on the small table. Good night, sir."

CONCEALED ART

IF a fellow has lots of money and lots of time and lots of curiosity about other fellows' business, it is astonishing, don't you know, what a lot of strange affairs he can get mixed up in. Now, I have money and curiosity and all the time there is. My name's Pepper – Reggie Pepper. My uncle was the colliery-owner chappie, and he left me the dickens of a pile. And ever since the lawyer slipped the stuff into my hand, whispering "It's yours!" life seems to have been one thing after another.

For instance, the dashed rummy case of dear old Archie. I first ran into old Archie when he was studying in Paris, and when he came back to London he looked me up, and we celebrated. He always liked me because I didn't mind listening to his theories of Art. For Archie, you must know, was an artist. Not an ordinary artist either, but one of those fellows you read about who are several years ahead of the times, and paint the sort of thing that people will be educated up to by about 1999 or thereabouts.

Well, one day as I was sitting in the club watching the traffic coming up one way and going down the other, and thinking nothing in particular, in blew the old boy. He was looking rather worried.

"Reggie, I want your advice."

"You shall have it," I said. "State your point, old top."

"It's like this – I'm engaged to be married."

"My dear old scout, a million con—"

"Yes, I know. Thanks very much, and all that, but listen."

"What's the trouble? Don't you like her?"

A kind of rapt expression came over his face.

"Like her! Why, she's the only—"

He gibbered for a spell. When he had calmed down, I said, "Well then, what's your trouble?"

"Reggie," he said, "do you think a man is bound to tell his wife all about his past life?"

"Oh, well," I said, "of course, I suppose she's prepared to find that a man has – er – sowed his wild oats, don't you know, and all that sort of thing, and—"

He seemed quite irritated.

"Don't be a chump. It's nothing like that. Listen. When I came back to London and started to try and make a living by painting, I found that people simply wouldn't buy the sort of work I did at any price. Do you know, Reggie, I've been at it three years now, and I haven't sold a single picture."

I whooped in a sort of amazed way, but I should have been far more startled if he'd told me he *had* sold a picture. I've seen his pictures, and they are like nothing on earth. So far as I can make out what he says, they aren't supposed to be. There's one in particular, called "The Coming of Summer," which I sometimes dream about when I've been hitting it up a shade too vigorously. It's all dots and splashes, with a great eye staring out of the middle of the mess. It looks as if summer, just as it was on the way, had stubbed its toe on a bomb. He tells me it's his masterpiece, and that he will never do anything like it again. I should like to have that in writing.

"Well, artists eat, just the same as other people," he went on, "and personally I like mine often and well cooked. Besides which, my sojourn in Paris gave me a rather nice taste in light wines. The consequence was that I came to the conclusion, after I had been back a few months, that something had to be done. Reggie, do you by any remote chance read a paper called *Funny Slices?*"

"Every week."

He gazed at me with a kind of wistful admiration.

"I envy you, Reggie. Fancy being able to make a statement like that openly and without fear. Then I take it you know the Doughnut family?"

"I should say I did."

His voice sank almost to a whisper, and he looked over his shoulder nervously.

"Reggie, I do them."

"You what?"

"I do them – draw them – paint them. I am the creator of the Doughnut family."

I stared at him, absolutely astounded. I was simply dumb. It was the biggest surprise of my life. Why, dash it, the Doughnut family was the best thing in its line in London. There is Pa Doughnut, Ma Doughnut, Aunt Bella, Cousin Joe, and Mabel, the daughter, and they have all sorts of slapstick adventures. Pa, Ma and Aunt Bella are pure gargoyles; Cousin Joe is a little more nearly semi-human, and Mabel is a perfect darling. I had often wondered who did them, for they were unsigned, and I had often thought what a deuced brainy fellow the chap must be. And all the time it was old Archie. I stammered as I tried to congratulate him.

He winced.

"Don't gargle, Reggie, there's a good fellow," he said. "My nerves are all on edge. Well, as I say, I do the Doughnuts. It was that or starvation. I got the idea one night when I had a toothache, and next day I took some specimens round to an editor. He rolled in his chair, and told me to start in and go on till further notice. Since then I have done them without a break. Well, there's the position. I must go on drawing these infernal things, or I shall be penniless. The question is, am I to tell her?"

"Tell her? Of course you must tell her."

"Ah, but you don't know her, Reggie. Have you ever heard of Eunice Nugent?"

"Not to my knowledge."

"As she doesn't sprint up and down the joyway at the Hippodrome, I didn't suppose you would."

I thought this rather uncalled-for, seeing that, as a matter of fact, I scarcely know a dozen of the Hippodrome chorus, but I made allowances for his state of mind.

"She's a poetess," he went on, "and her work has appeared in lots of good magazines. My idea is that she would be utterly horrified if she knew, and could never be quite the same to me again. But I want you to meet her and judge for yourself. It's just possible that I am taking too morbid a view of the matter, and I want an unprejudiced outside opinion. Come and lunch with us at the Piccadilly tomorrow, will you?"

He was absolutely right. One glance at Miss Nugent told me that the poor old boy had got the correct idea. I hardly know how to describe the impression she made on me. On the way to the Pic, Archie had told me that what first attracted him to her was the fact that she was so utterly unlike Mabel Doughnut; but that had not prepared me for what she really was. She was kind of intense, if you know what I mean – kind of spiritual. She was perfectly pleasant, and drew me out about golf and all that sort of thing; but all the time I felt that she considered me an earthy worm whose loftier soul-essence had been carelessly left out of his composition at birth. She made me wish that I had never seen a musical comedy or danced on a supper table on New Year's Eve. And if that was the impression she made on me, you can understand why poor old Archie jibbed at the idea of bringing her *Funny Slices*, and pointing at the Doughnuts and saying, "Me – I did it!" The notion was absolutely out of the question. The shot wasn't on the board. I told Archie so directly we were alone.

"Old top," I said, "you must keep it dark."

"I'm afraid so. But I hate the thought of deceiving her."

"You must get used to that now you're going to be a married man," I said.

"The trouble is, how am I going to account for the fact that I can do myself pretty well?"

"Why, tell her you have private means, of course. What's your money invested in?"

"Practically all of it in B. and O. P. Rails. It is a devilish good thing. A pal of mine put me onto it."

"Tell her that you have a pile of money in B. and O. P., then. She'll take it for granted it's a legacy. A spiritual girl like Miss Nugent isn't likely to inquire further."

"Reggie, I believe you're right. It cuts both ways, that spiritual gag. I'll do it."

❦

They were married quietly. I held the towel for Archie, and a spectacled girl with a mouth like a rat-trap, who was something to do with the Woman's Movement, saw fair play for Eunice. And then they went off to Scotland for their honeymoon. I wondered how the Doughnuts were going to get on in old Archie's absence, but it seemed that he had buckled down to it and turned out three months' supply in advance. He told me that long practice had enabled him to Doughnut almost without conscious effort. When he came back to London he would give an hour a week to them and do them on his head. Pretty soft! It seemed to me that the marriage was going to be a success.

One gets out of touch with people when they marry. I am not much on the social-call game, and for nearly six months I don't suppose I saw Archie more than twice or three times. When I did, he appeared sound in wind and limb, and reported that married life was all to the velvet, and that he regarded bachelors like myself as so many excrescences on the social system. He compared me, if I remember rightly, to a wart, and advocated drastic treatment.

It was perhaps seven months after he had told Eunice that he endowed her with all his worldly goods – she not suspecting what the parcel contained – that he came to me unexpectedly one afternoon with a face so long and sick-looking that my finger was on the button and I was ordering brandy and soda before he had time to speak.

"Reggie," he said, "an awful thing has happened. Have you seen the paper today?"

"Yes. Why?"

"Did you read the Stock Exchange news? Did you see that some lunatic has been jumping around with a club and hammering the stuffing out of B. and O. P.? This afternoon they are worth practically nothing."

"By jove! And all your money was in it. What rotten luck!" Then I spotted the silver lining. "But, after all, it doesn't matter so very much. What I mean is, bang go your little savings and all that sort of thing; but, after all, you're making quite a good income, so why worry?"

"I might have known you would miss the point," he said. "Can't you understand the situation? This morning at breakfast Eunice got hold of the paper first. 'Archie,' she said, 'didn't you tell me all your money was in B. and O. P.?' 'Yes,' I said. 'Why?' 'Then we're ruined.' Now do you see? If I had had time to think, I could have said that I had another chunk in something else, but I had committed myself, I have either got to tell her about those infernal Doughnuts, or else conceal the fact that I had money coming in."

"Great Scot! What on earth are you going to do?"

"I can't think. We can struggle along in a sort of way, for it appears that she has small private means of her own. The idea at present is that we shall live on them. We're selling the car, and trying to get out of the rest of our lease up at the flat, and then we're going to look about for a cheaper place, probably down Chelsea way, so as to be near my studio. What was that stuff I've been drinking? Ring for another of the same, there's a good fellow. In fact, I think you had better keep your finger permanently on the bell. I shall want all they've got."

The spectacle of a fellow human being up to his neck in the consommé is painful, of course, but there's certainly what the advertisements at the top of magazine stories call a "tense human interest" about it, and I'm bound to say that I saw as much as possible of poor old Archie from now on. His sad case fascinated me. It was rather thrilling to see him wrestling with New Zealand mutton-hash and draught beer down at his Chelsea flat, with all the suppressed anguish of a man who has let himself get accustomed to delicate food and vintage wines, and think that a word from him could send him whizzing back to the old life again whenever he wished. But at what a cost, as they say in the novels. That was the catch. He might hate this new order of things, but his lips were sealed.

I personally came in for a good deal of quiet esteem for the way in which I stuck to him in his adversity. I don't think Eunice had thought much of me before, but now she seemed to feel that I had formed a corner in golden hearts. I took advantage of this to try and pave the way for a confession on poor old Archie's part.

"I wonder, Archie, old top," I said one evening after we had dined on mutton-hash and were sitting round trying to forget it, "I wonder you don't try another line in painting. I've heard that some of these fellows who draw for the comic papers—"

Mrs. Archie nipped me in the bud.

"How can you suggest such a thing, Mr. Pepper? A man with Archie's genius! I know the public is not educated up to his work, but it is only a question of time. Archie suffers, like all pioneers, from being ahead of his generation. But, thank Heaven, he need not sully his genius by stooping—"

"No, no," I said. "Sorry. I only suggested it."

After that I gave more time than ever to trying to think of a solution. Sometimes I would lie awake at night, and my manner towards Wilberforce, my man, became so distrait that it almost caused a rift. He asked me one morning which suit I would wear that day, and, by Jove, I said, "Oh, any of them. I don't mind." There was a most frightful silence, and I woke up to find him looking at me with such a dashed wounded expression in his eyes that I had to tip him a couple of quid to bring him round again.

Well, you can't go on straining your brain like that forever without something breaking loose, and one night, just after I had gone to bed, I got it. Yes, by gad, absolutely got it. And I was so excited that I hopped out from under the blankets there and then, and rang up old Archie on the phone.

"Archie, old scout," I said, "can the misses hear what I'm saying? Well then, don't say anything to give the show away. Keep on saying, 'Yes? Halloa?' so that you can tell her it was someone on the wrong wire. I've got it, my boy. All you've got to do to solve the whole problem is to tell her you've sold one of your pictures. Make the price as big as you like. Come and lunch with me tomorrow at the club, and we'll settle the details."

There was a pause, and then Archie's voice said, "Halloa, halloa?" It might have been a bit disappointing, only there was a tremble in it which made me understand how happy I had made the old boy. I went back to bed and slept like a king.

Next day we lunched together, and fixed the thing up. I have never seen anyone so supremely braced. We examined the scheme from every angle and there wasn't a flaw in it. The only difficulty was to hit on a plausible purchaser. Archie suggested me, but I couldn't see it. I said it would sound fishy. Eventually I had a brain wave, and suggested J. Bellingwood Brackett, the American millionaire. He lives in London, and you see his name in the papers everyday as having bought some painting or statue or something, so why shouldn't he buy Archie's "Coming of Summer?" And Archie said, "Exactly – why shouldn't he? And if he had had any sense in his fat head, he would have done it long ago, dash him!" Which shows you that dear old Archie was bracing up, for I've heard him use much the same language in happier days about a referee.

He went off, crammed to the eyebrows with good food and happiness, to tell Mrs. Archie that all was well, and that the old home was saved, and that Canterbury mutton might now be definitely considered as off the bill of fare.

He told me on the phone that night that he had made the price two thousand pounds, because he needed the money, and what was two thousand to a man who had been fleecing the widow and the orphan for forty odd years without a break? I thought the price was a bit high, but I agreed that J. Bellingwood could afford it. And happiness, you might say, reigned supreme.

I don't know when I've had such a nasty jar as I got when Wilberforce brought me the paper in bed, and I languidly opened it and this jumped out and bit at me:

BELLINGWOOD BRACKETT DISCOVERS ENGLISH GENIUS
PAYS STUPENDOUS PRICE FOR YOUNG ARTIST'S PICTURE
HITHERTO UNKNOWN FUTURIST RECEIVED 2,000 POUNDS

Underneath there was a column, some of it about Archie, the rest about the picture; and scattered over the page were two photographs of old Archie, looking more like Pa Doughnut than anything human, and a smudged reproduction of "The Coming of Summer"; and, believe me, frightful as the original of that weird exhibit looked, the reproduction had it licked to a whisper. It was one of the ghastliest things I have ever seen.

Well, after the first shock I recovered a bit. After all, it was fame for dear old Archie. As soon as I had had lunch I went down to the flat to congratulate him.

He was sitting there with Mrs. Archie. He was looking a bit dazed, but she was simmering with joy. She welcomed me as the faithful friend.

"Isn't it perfectly splendid, Mr. Pepper, to think that Archie's genius has at last been recognized? How quiet he kept it. I had no idea that Mr. Brackett was even interested in his work. I wonder how he heard of it?"

"Oh, these things get about," I said. "You can't keep a good man down."

"Think of two thousand pounds for one picture – and the first he has ever sold!"

"What beats me," I said, "is how the papers got hold of it."

"Oh, I sent it to the papers," said Mrs. Archie, in an offhand way.

"I wonder who did the writing up," I said.

"They would do that in the office, wouldn't they?" said Mrs. Archie.

"I suppose they would," I said. "They are wonders at that sort of thing."

I couldn't help wishing that Archie would enter into the spirit of the thing a little more and perk up, instead of sitting there looking like a codfish. The thing seemed to have stunned the poor chappie.

"After this, Archie," I said, "all you have to do is to sit in your studio, while the police see that the waiting line of millionaires doesn't straggle over the pavement. They'll fight—"

"What's that?" said Archie, starting as if someone had dug a red-hot needle into his calf.

It was only a ring at the bell, followed by a voice asking if Mr. Ferguson was at home.

"Probably an interviewer," said Mrs. Archie. "I suppose we shall get no peace for a long time to come."

The door opened, and the cook came in with a card. "'Renshaw Liggett,'" said Mrs. Archie "I don't know him. Do you, Archie? It must be an interviewer. Ask him to come in, Julia."

And in he came.

My knowledge of chappies in general, after a fairly wide experience, is that some chappies seem to kind of convey an atmosphere of unpleasantness the moment you come into contact with them. Renshaw Liggett gave me this feeling directly he came in; and when he fixed me with a sinister glance and said, "Mr. Ferguson?" I felt inclined to say "Not guilty." I backed a step or two and jerked my head towards Archie, and Renshaw turned the searchlight off me and switched it onto him.

"You are Mr. Archibald Ferguson, the artist?"

Archie nodded pallidly, and Renshaw nodded, as much as to say that you couldn't deceive him. He produced a sheet of paper. It was the middle page of the *Mail*.

"You authorized the publication of this?"

Archie nodded again.

"I represent Mr. Brackett. The publication of this most impudent fiction has caused Mr. Brackett extreme annoyance, and, as it might also lead to other and more serious consequences, I must insist that a full denial be published without a moment's delay."

"What do you mean?" cried Mrs. Archie. "Are you mad?"

She had been standing, listening to the conversation in a sort of trance. Now she jumped into the fight with a vim that turned Renshaw's attention to her in a second.

"No, madam, I am not mad. Nor, despite the interested assertions of certain parties whom I need not specify by name, is Mr. Brackett. It may be news to you, Mrs. Ferguson, that an action is even now pending in New York, whereby certain parties are attempting to show that my client, Mr. Brackett, is non compos and should be legally restrained from exercising control over his property. Their case is extremely weak, for even if we admit their contention that our client did, on the eighteenth of June last, attempt to walk up Fifth Avenue in his pyjamas, we shall be able to show that his action was the result of an election bet. But as the parties to whom I have alluded will undoubtedly snatch at every straw in their efforts to prove that Mr. Brackett is mentally infirm, the prejudicial effect of this publication cannot be over-estimated. Unless Mr. Brackett can clear himself of the stigma of having given two thousand pounds for this extraordinary production of an absolutely unknown artist, the strength of his case must be seriously shaken. I may add that my client's lavish patronage of Art is already one of the main planks in the platform of the parties already referred to. They adduce his extremely generous expenditure in this direction as evidence that he is incapable of a proper handling of his money. I need scarcely point out with what sinister pleasure, therefore, they must have contemplated – this."

And he looked at "The Coming of Summer" as if it were a black beetle.

I must say, much as I disliked the blighter, I couldn't help feeling that he had right on his side. It hadn't occurred to me in quite that light before, but, considering it calmly now, I could see that a man who would disgorge two thousand of the best for Archie's Futurist masterpiece might very well step straight into the nut factory, and no questions asked.

Mrs. Archie came right back at him, as game as you please.

"I am sorry for Mr. Brackett's domestic troubles, but my husband can prove without difficulty that he did buy the picture. Can't you, dear?"

Archie, extremely white about the gills, looked at the ceiling and at the floor and at me and Renshaw Liggett.

"No," he said finally. "I can't. Because he didn't."

"Exactly," said Renshaw, "and I must ask you to publish that statement in tomorrow's papers without fail." He rose, and made for the door. "My client has no objection to young artists advertising themselves, realizing that this is an age of strenuous competition, but he firmly refuses to permit them to do it at his expense. Good afternoon."

And he legged it, leaving behind him one of the most chunky silences I have ever been mixed up in. For the life of me, I couldn't see who was to make the next remark. I was jolly certain that it wasn't going to be me.

Eventually Mrs. Archie opened the proceedings.

"What does it mean?"

Archie turned to me with a sort of frozen calm.

"Reggie, would you mind stepping into the kitchen and asking Julia for this week's *Funny Slices?* I know she has it."

He was right. She unearthed it from a cupboard. I trotted back with it to the sitting room. Archie took the paper from me, and held it out to his wife, Doughnuts uppermost.

"Look!" he said.

She looked.

"I do them. I have done them every week for three years. No, don't speak yet. Listen. This is where all my money came from, all the money I lost when B. and O. P. Rails went smash. And this is where the money came from to buy 'The Coming of Summer.' It wasn't Brackett who bought it; it was myself."

Mrs. Archie was devouring the Doughnuts with wide-open eyes. I caught a glimpse of them myself, and only just managed not to laugh, for it was the set of pictures where Pa Doughnut tries to fix the electric light, one of the very finest things dear old Archie had ever done.

"I don't understand," she said.

"I draw these things. I have sold my soul."

"Archie!"

He winced, but stuck to it bravely.

"Yes, I knew how you would feel about it, and that was why I didn't dare to tell you, and why we fixed up this story about old Brackett.

I couldn't bear to live on you any longer, and to see you roughing it here, when we might be having all the money we wanted."

Suddenly, like a boiler exploding, she began to laugh.

"They're the funniest things I ever saw in my life," she gurgled. "Mr. Pepper, do look! He's trying to cut the electric wire with the scissors, and everything blazes up. And you've been hiding this from me all that time!"

Archie goggled dumbly. She dived at a table, and picked up a magazine, pointing to one of the advertisement pages.

"Read!" she cried. "Read it aloud."

And in a shaking voice Archie read:

You think you are perfectly well, don't you? You wake up in the morning and spring out of bed and say to yourself that you have never been better in your life. You're wrong! Unless you are avoiding coffee as you would avoid the man who always tells you the smart things his little boy said yesterday, and drinking SAFETY FIRST MOLASSINE for breakfast, you cannot be Perfectly Well.

It is a physical impossibility. Coffee contains an appreciable quantity of the deadly drug caffeine, and therefore—

"I wrote *that*," she said. "And I wrote the advertisement of the Spiller Baby Food on page ninety-four, and the one about the Pre-eminent Breakfast Sausage on page eighty-six. Oh, Archie, dear, the torments I have been through, fearing that you would some day find me out and despise me. I couldn't help it. I had no private means, and I didn't make enough out of my poetry to keep me in hats. I learned to write advertisements four years ago at a correspondence school, and I've been doing them ever since. And now I don't mind your knowing, now that you have told me this perfectly splendid news. Archie!"

She rushed into his arms like someone charging in for a bowl of soup at a railway station buffet. And I drifted out. It seemed to me that this was a scene in which I was not on. I sidled to the door, and slid forth. They didn't notice me. My experience is that nobody ever does – much.

THE TEST CASE

WELL-MEANING chappies at the club sometimes amble up to me and tap me on the wishbone, and say "Reggie, old top," – my name's Reggie Pepper – "you ought to get married, old man." Well, what I mean to say is, it's all very well, and I see their point and all that sort of thing; but it takes two to make a marriage, and to date I haven't met a girl who didn't seem to think the contract was too big to be taken on.

Looking back, it seems to me that I came nearer to getting over the home-plate with Ann Selby than with most of the others. In fact, but for circumstances over which I had no dashed control, I am inclined to think that we should have brought it off. I'm bound to say that, now that what the poet chappie calls the first fine frenzy has been on the ice for awhile and I am able to consider the thing calmly, I am deuced glad we didn't. She was one of those strong-minded girls, and I hate to think of what she would have done to me.

At the time, though, I was frightfully in love, and, for quite a while after she definitely gave me the mitten, I lost my stroke at golf so completely that a child could have given me a stroke a hole and got away with it. I was all broken up, and I contend to this day that I was dashed badly treated.

Let me give you what they call the data.

One day I was lunching with Ann, and was just proposing to her as usual, when, instead of simply refusing me, as she generally did, she fixed me with a thoughtful eye and kind of opened her heart.

"Do you know, Reggie, I am in doubt."

"Give me the benefit of it," I said. Which I maintain was pretty good on the spur of the moment, but didn't get a hand. She simply ignored it, and went on.

"Sometimes," she said, "you seem to me entirely vapid and brainless; at other times you say or do things which suggest that there are possibilities in you; that, properly stimulated and encouraged, you might overcome the handicap of large private means and do something worthwhile. I wonder if that is simply my imagination?" She watched me very closely as she spoke.

"Rather not. You've absolutely summed me up. With you beside me, stimulating and all that sort of rot, don't you know, I should show a flash of speed which would astonish you."

"I wish I could be certain."

"Take a chance on it."

She shook her head.

"I must be certain. Marriage is such a gamble. I have just been staying with my sister Hilda and her husband—"

"Dear old Harold Bodkin. I know him well. In fact, I've a standing invitation to go down there and stay as long as I like. Harold is one of my best pals. Harold is a corker. Good old Harold is—"

"I would rather you didn't eulogize him, Reggie. I am extremely angry with Harold. He is making Hilda perfectly miserable."

"What on earth do you mean? Harold wouldn't dream of hurting a fly. He's one of those dreamy, sentimental chumps who—"

"It is precisely his sentimentality which is at the bottom of the whole trouble. You know, of course, that Hilda is not his first wife?"

"That's right. His first wife died about five years ago."

"He still cherishes her memory."

"Very sporting of him."

"Is it! If you were a girl, how would you like to be married to a man who was always making you bear in mind that you were only number two in his affections; a man whose idea of a pleasant conversation was a string of anecdotes illustrating what a dear woman his first wife was. A man who expected you to upset all your plans if they clashed with some anniversary connected with his other marriage?"

"That does sound pretty rotten. Does Harold do all that?"

"That's only a small part of what he does. Why, if you will believe me, every evening at seven o'clock he goes and shuts himself up in a little room at the top of the house, and meditates."

"What on earth does he do that for?"

"Apparently his first wife died at seven in the evening. There is a portrait of her in the room. I believe he lays flowers in front of it. And Hilda is expected to greet him on his return with a happy smile."

"Why doesn't she kick?"

"I have been trying to persuade her to, but she won't. She just pretends she doesn't mind. She has a nervous, sensitive temperament, and the thing is slowly crushing her. Don't talk to me of Harold."

Considering that she had started him as a topic, I thought this pretty unjust. I didn't want to talk of Harold. I wanted to talk about myself.

"Well, what has all this got to do with your not wanting to marry me?" I said.

"Nothing, except that it is an illustration of the risks a woman runs when she marries a man of a certain type."

"Great Scott! You surely don't class me with Harold?"

"Yes, in a way you are very much alike. You have both always had large private means, and have never had the wholesome discipline of work."

"But, dash it, Harold, on your showing, is an absolute nut. Why should you think that I would be anything like that?"

"There's always the risk."

A hot idea came to me.

"Look here, Ann," I said, "Suppose I pull off some stunt which only a deuced brainy chappie could get away with? Would you marry me then?"

"Certainly. What do you propose to do?"

"Do! What do I propose to do! Well, er, to be absolutely frank, at the moment I don't quite know."

"You never will know, Reggie. You're one of the idle rich, and your brain, if you ever had one, has atrophied."

Well, that seemed to me to put the lid on it. I didn't mind a heart-to-heart talk, but this was mere abuse. I changed the subject.

"What would you like after that fish?" I said coldly.

You know how it is when you get an idea. For awhile it sort of simmers inside you, and then suddenly it sizzles up like a rocket, and there you are, right up against it. That's what happened now. I went away from that luncheon, vaguely determined to pull off some stunt which would prove that I was right there with the gray matter, but without any clear notion of what I was going to do. Side by side with this in my mind was the case of dear old Harold. When I wasn't brooding on the stunt, I was brooding on Harold. I was fond of the good old lad, and I hated the idea of his slowly wrecking the home purely by being a chump. And all of a sudden the two things clicked together like a couple of chemicals, and there I was with a corking plan for killing two birds with one stone – putting one across that would startle and impress Ann, and at the same time healing the breach between Harold and Hilda.

My idea was that, in a case like this, it's no good trying opposition. What you want is to work it so that the chappie quits of his own accord. You want to egg him on to overdoing the thing till he gets so that he says to himself, "Enough! Never again!" That was what was going to happen to Harold.

When you're going to do a thing, there's nothing like making a quick start. I wrote to Harold straight away, proposing myself for a visit. And Harold wrote back telling me to come right along.

Harold and Hilda lived alone in a large house. I believe they did a good deal of entertaining at times, but on this occasion I was the only guest. The only other person of note in the place was Ponsonby, the butler.

Of course, if Harold had been an ordinary sort of chappie, what I had come to do would have been a pretty big order. I don't mind many things, but I do hesitate to dig into my host's intimate private affairs. But Harold was such a simple-minded Johnnie, so grateful for a little sympathy and advice, that my job wasn't so very difficult.

It wasn't as if he minded talking about Amelia, which was his first wife's name. The difficulty was to get him to talk of anything else. I began to understand what Ann meant by saying it was tough on Hilda.

I'm bound to say the old boy was clay in my hands. People call me a chump, but Harold was a super-chump, and I did what I liked with him. The second morning of my visit, after breakfast, he grabbed me by the arm.

"This way, Reggie. I'm just going to show old Reggie Amelia's portrait, dear."

There was a little room all by itself on the top floor. He explained to me that it had been his studio. At one time Harold used to do a bit of painting in an amateur way.

"There!" he said, pointing at the portrait. "I did that myself, Reggie. It was away being cleaned when you were here last. It's like dear Amelia, isn't it?"

I suppose it was, in a way. At any rate, you could recognize the likeness when you were told who it was supposed to be.

He sat down in front of it, and gave it the thoughtful once-over.

"Do you know, Reggie, old top, sometimes when I sit here, I feel as if Amelia were back again."

"It would be a bit awkward for you if she was."

"How do you mean?"

"Well, old lad, you happen to be married to someone else."

A look of childlike enthusiasm came over his face.

"Reggie, I want to tell you how splendid Hilda is. Lots of other women might object to my still cherishing Amelia's memory, but Hilda has been so nice about it from the beginning. She understands so thoroughly."

I hadn't much breath left after that, but I used what I had to say: "She doesn't object?"

"Not a bit," said Harold. "It makes everything so pleasant."

When I had recovered a bit, I said, "What do you mean by everything?"

"Well," he said, "for instance, I come up here every evening at seven and – er – think for a few minutes."

"A few minutes?!"

"What do you mean?"

"Well, a few minutes isn't long."

"But I always have my cocktail at a quarter past."

"You could postpone it."

"And Ponsonby likes us to start dinner at seven-thirty."

"What on earth has Ponsonby to do with it?"

"Well, he likes to get off by nine, you know. I think he goes off and plays bowls at the madhouse. You see, Reggie, old man, we have to study Ponsonby a little. He's always on the verge of giving notice – in fact, it was only by coaxing him on one or two occasions that we got him to stay on – and he's such a treasure that I don't know what we should do if we lost him. But, if you think that I ought to stay longer—?"

"Certainly I do. You ought to do a thing like this properly, or not at all."

He sighed.

"It's a frightful risk, but in future we'll dine at eight."

It seemed to me that there was a suspicion of a cloud on Ponsonby's shining morning face, when the news was broken to him that for the future he couldn't unleash himself on the local bowling talent as early as usual, but he made no kick, and the new order of things began.

My next offensive movement I attribute to a flash of absolute genius. I was glancing through a photograph album in the drawing-room before lunch, when I came upon a face which I vaguely remembered. It was one of those wide, flabby faces, with bulging eyes, and something about it struck me as familiar. I consulted Harold, who came in at that moment.

"That?" said Harold. "That's Percy." He gave a slight shudder. "Amelia's brother, you know. An awful fellow. I haven't seen him for years."

Then I placed Percy. I had met him once or twice in the old days, and I had a brainwave. Percy was everything that poor old Harold disliked most. He was hearty at breakfast, a confirmed back-slapper, and a man who prodded you in the chest when he spoke to you.

"You haven't seen him for years!" I said in a shocked voice.

"Thank heaven!" said Harold devoutly.

I put down the photograph album, and looked at him in a deuced serious way. "Then it's high time you asked him to come here."

Harold blanched. "Reggie, old man, you don't know what you are saying. You can't remember Percy. I wish you wouldn't say these things, even in fun."

"I'm not saying it in fun. Of course, it's none of my business, but you have paid me the compliment of confiding in me about Amelia, and I feel justified in speaking. All I can say is that, if you cherish her memory as you say you do, you show it in a very strange way. How you can square your neglect of Percy with your alleged devotion to Amelia's memory, beats me. It seems to me that you have no choice. You must either drop the whole thing and admit that your love for her is dead, or else you must stop this infernal treatment of her favorite brother. You can't have it both ways."

He looked at me like a hunted stag. "But, Reggie, old man! Percy! He asks riddles at breakfast."

"I don't care."

"Hilda can't stand him."

"It doesn't matter. You must invite him. It's not a case of what you like or don't like. It's your duty."

He struggled with his feelings for a bit. "Very well," he said in a crushed sort of voice.

At dinner that night he said to Hilda: "I'm going to ask Amelia's brother down to spend a few days. It is so long since we have seen him."

Hilda didn't answer at once. She looked at him in rather a curious sort of way, I thought. "Very well, dear," she said.

I was deuced sorry for the poor girl, but I felt like a surgeon. She would be glad later on, for I was convinced that in a very short while poor old Harold must crack under the strain, especially after I had put across the coup which I was meditating for the very next evening.

It was quite simple. Simple, that is to say, in its working, but a devilish brainy thing for a chappie to have thought out. If Ann had really meant what she had said at lunch that day, and was prepared to stick to her bargain and marry me as soon as I showed a burst of intelligence, she was mine.

What it came to was that, if dear old Harold enjoyed meditating in front of Amelia's portrait, he was jolly well going to have all the meditating he wanted, and a bit over, for my simple scheme was to lurk outside till he had gone into the little room on the top floor, and then, with the aid of one of those jolly little wedges which you use to keep windows from rattling, see to it that the old boy remained there till they sent out search parties.

There wasn't a flaw in my reasoning. When Harold didn't roll in at the sound of the dinner gong, Hilda would take it for granted that he was doing an extra bit of meditating that night, and her pride would stop her sending out a hurry call for him. As for Harold, when he found that all was not well with the door, he would probably yell with considerable vim. But it was odds against anyone hearing him. As for me, you might think that I was going to suffer owing to the probable postponement of dinner. Not so, but far otherwise, for on the night I had selected for the coup I was dining out at the neighboring inn with my old college chum Freddie Meadowes. It is true that Freddie wasn't going to be within fifty miles of the place on that particular night, but they weren't to know that.

Did I describe the peculiar isolation of that room on the top floor, where the portrait was? I don't think I did. It was, as a matter of fact, the only room in those parts, for, in the days when he did his amateur painting, old Harold was strong on the artistic seclusion business and hated noise, and his studio was the only room in use on that floor.

In short, to sum up, the thing was a cinch.

Punctually at ten minutes to seven, I was in readiness on the scene. There was a recess with a curtain in front of it a few yards from the door, and there I waited, fondling my little wedge, for Harold to walk up and allow the proceedings to start. It was almost pitch-dark, and that made the time of waiting seem longer. Presently – I seemed to have been there longer than ten minutes – I heard steps approaching. They came past where I stood, and went on into the room. The door closed, and I hopped out and sprinted up to it, and the next moment I had the good old wedge under the wood – as neat a job as you could imagine. And then I strolled downstairs, and toddled off to the inn.

I didn't hurry over my dinner, partly because the browsing and sluicing at the inn was really astonishingly good for a roadhouse and partly because I wanted to give Harold plenty of time for meditation. I suppose it must have been a couple of hours or more when I finally turned in at the front door. Somebody was playing the piano in the drawing room. It could only be Hilda who was playing, and I had doubts as to whether she wanted company just then – mine, at any rate.

Eventually I decided to risk it, for I wanted to hear the latest about dear old Harold, so in I went, and it wasn't Hilda at all; it was Ann Selby.

"Hello," I said. "I didn't know you were coming down here." It seemed so odd, don't you know, as it hadn't been more than ten days or so since her last visit.

"Good evening, Reggie," she said.

"What's been happening?" I asked.

"How do you know anything has been happening?"

"I guessed it."

"Well, you're quite right, as it happens, Reggie. A good deal has been happening." She went to the door, and looked out, listening. Then she shut it, and came back. "Hilda has revolted!"

"Revolted?"

"Yes, put her foot down – made a stand – refused to go on meekly putting up with Harold's insane behavior."

"I don't understand."

She gave me a look of pity. "You always were so dense, Reggie. I will tell you the whole thing from the beginning. You remember what I spoke to you about, one day when we were lunching together? Well, I don't suppose you have noticed it – I know what you are – but things have been getting steadily worse. For one thing, Harold insisted on lengthening his visits to the top room, and naturally Ponsonby complained. Hilda tells me that she had to plead with him to induce him to stay on. Then the climax came. I don't know if you recollect Amelia's brother Percy? You must have met him when she was alive – a perfectly unspeakable person with a loud voice and overpowering manners. Suddenly, out of a blue sky, Harold announced his intention of inviting him to stay. It was the last straw. This afternoon I received a telegram from poor Hilda, saying that she was leaving Harold and coming to stay with me, and a few hours later the poor child arrived at my apartment."

You mustn't suppose that I stood listening silently to this speech. Every time she seemed to be going to stop for breath I tried to horn in and tell her all these things which had been happening were not mere flukes, as she seemed to think, but parts of a deuced carefully planned scheme of my own. Every time I'd try to interrupt, Ann would wave me down, and carry on without so much as a semi-colon.

But at this point I did manage a word in. "I know, I know, I know! I did it all. It was I who suggested to Harold that he should lengthen the meditations, and insisted on his inviting Percy to stay."

I had hardly got the words out, when I saw that they were not making the hit I had anticipated. She looked at me with an expression of absolute scorn, don't you know.

"Well, really, Reggie," she said at last, "I never have had a very high opinion of your intelligence, as you know, but this is a revelation to me. What motive you can have had, unless you did it in a spirit of pure mischief—" She stopped, and there was a glare of undiluted repulsion in her eyes. "Reggie! I can't believe it! Of all the things I loathe most, a practical joker is the worst. Do you mean to tell me you did all this as a practical joke?"

"Great Scott, no! It was like this—"

I paused for a bare second to collect my thoughts, so as to put the thing clearly to her. I might have known what would happen. She dashed right in and collared the conversation.

"Well, never mind. As it happens, there is no harm done. Quite the reverse, in fact. Hilda left a note for Harold telling him what she had done and where she had gone and why she had gone, and Harold found it. The result was that, after Hilda had been with me for some time, in he came in a panic and absolutely grovelled before the dear child. It seems incredible but he had apparently had no notion that his absurd behavior had met with anything but approval from Hilda. He went on as if he were mad. He was beside himself. He clutched his hair and stamped about the room, and then he jumped at the telephone and called this house and got Ponsonby and told him to go straight to the little room on the top floor and take Amelia's portrait down. I thought that a little unnecessary myself, but he was in such a whirl of remorse that it was useless to try and get him to be rational. So Hilda was consoled, and he calmed down, and we all came down here in the automobile. So you see—"

At this moment the door opened, and in came Harold.

"I say – hello, Reggie, old man – I say, it's a funny thing, but we can't find Ponsonby anywhere."

There are moments in a chappie's life, don't you know, when Reason, so to speak, totters, as it were, on its bally throne. This was one of them. The situation seemed somehow to have got out of my grip. I suppose, strictly speaking, I ought, at this juncture, to have cleared my throat and said in an audible tone, "Harold, old top, *I* know where Ponsonby is." But somehow I couldn't. Something seemed to keep the words back. I just stood there and said nothing.

"Nobody seems to have seen anything of him," said Harold. "I wonder where he can have got to."

Hilda came in, looking so happy I hardly recognized her. I remember feeling how strange it was that anybody could be happy just then.

"*I* know," she said. "Of course! Doesn't he always go off to the inn and play bowls at this time?"

"Why, of course," said Harold. "So he does."

And he asked Ann to play something on the piano. And pretty soon we had settled down to a regular jolly musical evening. Ann must have played a matter of two or three thousand tunes, when Harold got up.

"By the way," he said. "I suppose he did what I told him about the picture before he went out. Let's go and see."

"Oh, Harold, what does it matter?" asked Hilda.

"Don't be silly, Harold," said Ann.

I would have said the same thing, only I couldn't say anything.

Harold wasn't to be stopped. He led the way out of the room and upstairs, and we all trailed after him. We had just reached the top floor, when Hilda stopped, and said "Hark!"

It was a voice.

"Hi!" it said. "Hi!"

Harold legged it to the door of the studio. "Ponsonby?"

From within came the voice again, and I have never heard anything to touch the combined pathos, dignity and indignation it managed to condense into two words.

"Yes, sir?"

"What on earth are you doing in there?"

"I came here, sir, in accordance with your instructions on the telephone, and—"

Harold rattled the door. "The darned thing's stuck."

"Yes, sir."

"How on earth did that happen?"

"I could not say, sir."

"How *can* the door have stuck like this?" said Ann.

Somebody – I suppose it was me, though the voice didn't sound familiar – spoke. "Perhaps there's a wedge under it," said this chappie.

"A wedge? What do you mean?"

"One of those little wedges you use to keep windows from rattling, don't you know."

"But why—? You're absolutely right, Reggie, old man, there is!"

He yanked it out, and flung the door open, and out came Ponsonby, looking like Lady Macbeth.

"I wish to give notice, sir," he said, "and I should esteem it a favor if I might go to the pantry and procure some food, as I am extremely hungry."

And he passed from our midst, with Hilda after him, saying: "But, Ponsonby! Be reasonable, Ponsonby!"